Other books by Mark Timlin

A Good Year for the Roses 1988
Romeo's Girl 1990
Gun Street Girl 1990
Take the A-Train 1991
The Turnaround 1991
Zip Gun Boogie 1992
Hearts of Stone 1992
Falls the Shadow 1993
Ashes by Now 1993
Pretend We're Dead 1994
Paint It Black 1995
Find My Way Home 1996
Sharman and Other Filth (short stories) 1996
A Street That Rhymed with 3 AM 1997
Dead Flowers 1998
Quick Before They Catch Us 1999
All the Empty Places 2000
Stay Another Day 2010

OTHERS
I Spied a Pale Horse 1999
Answers from the Grave 2004
as TONY WILLIAMS
Valin's Raiders 1994
Blue on Blue 1999
as JIM BALLANTYNE
The Torturer 1995
as MARTIN MILK
That Saturday 1996
as LEE MARTIN
Gangsters Wives 2007
The Lipstick Killers 2009

mark timlin

zip gun boogie

The Sixth Nick Sharman Thriller

NO EXIT PRESS

This edition published in 2014
by No Exit Press,
an imprint of Oldcastle Books
P.O.Box 394, Harpenden,
Herts, AL5 1XJ, UK

noexit.co.uk
@NoExitPress

First published in 1992 by Headline Book Publishing plc

A CIP catalogue record for this book is available from the British Library.

ISBN
978-1-84344-273-8 (print)
978-1-84344-274-5 (epub)
978-1-84344-275-2 (kindle)
978-1-84344-276-9 (pdf)

Typeset by Avocet Typeset, Somerton, Somerset
in 11pt Garamond
Printed in Great Britain by Clays Ltd, St Ives plc

For more information about Crime Fiction go to crimetime.co.uk
@CrimeTimeUK

This one goes out to the one I love.

1

Tuesday morning, 11.55. Nothing doing. I'd read the papers and was sitting in my office, debating whether or not to go to lunch, when the telephone rang. I picked up the receiver. 'Nick Sharman,' I said.

'I was talking to Mark McBain a few weeks ago,' a male voice said in my ear. The accent was English, but with a strong American twang which placed it somewhere in the mid-Atlantic.

'He mentioned you,' the voice continued.

'Did he?' I said. 'How is he?'

'Good. You helped him a while back.'

It was a statement, rather than a question.

'That's right.'

'I called him up this morning and we talked some more.'

'Yes?' I said, hoping he'd get to the point.

'I told him I was going to call you. He sends his love.'

'That sounds like McBain.'

'He said for you to call him soon.'

'I will.'

'Have you got his number in LA?'

'Yes,' I said.

My caller fell silent.

'I presume that wasn't the only reason you rang?'

7

'What?'

'To pass on McBain's love.'

'No.'

'What then?'

'I wonder if you could help us?'

'Who's us?' I asked.

'*Pandora's Box.*'

'Didn't you have that album?'

'That's right,' said the voice. 'We had *that* album.'

The album in question was called *Regrets,* and until Michael Jackson came along with *Thriller,* it had been the biggest-selling long-playing record in history. 'What kind of help?' I asked.

'I think someone tried to murder one of the band last night.'

'Did they? I didn't see anything about it in the papers.'

'It hasn't been in the papers.'

'And who are you?'

'My name is Roger Lomax. I look after things for the band.'

'You're the manager?'

'They don't have a manager. Just a dozen lawyers, a firm of accountants and me. That's the way things go these days. Will you help?'

'I don't know what I can do.'

'Find out who tried to kill him.'

'What about the police?'

'No police.'

'Why's that?'

There was a long pause. 'I don't want to talk about it on the phone. I'd rather talk to you in person. I assure you it will be worth your while. Can we meet this afternoon?'

I wasn't doing anything. 'Sure,' I said. 'Where?'

'We're staying at Jones' Hotel in Knightsbridge. Do you know it?'

I didn't, but I was a detective. 'I'll find it.'

'Will you be driving?'

'Yes.'

'If you give me the registration number of your vehicle, I'll make sure you're cleared to park.'

I gave him the number.

'The parking is at the back of the hotel,' he told me. 'Follow the signs, see the guy at the gate. Is three o'clock convenient?'

'Sure.'

'I'll see you then,' he said, and hung up.

I replaced the receiver and went to lunch.

2

The hotel was located in a leafy avenue in Knightsbridge. There are still quite a few if you know where to look. It appeared to consist of a whole block of tall terraced town houses knocked into one. It had a new, green-tiled roof, the bricks had been scrubbed clean, and the paintwork sparkled in the sun. I drove slowly past the front entrance at 2.45 that afternoon. There was a gent in a brown uniform dripping with gold braid and wearing a brown top hat standing by the revolving door at the top of the stone steps that led up from the pavement. I kept going until I saw an illuminated sign that read: HOTEL PARKING, and an arrow that pointed to an arched alleyway that cut right through the hotel and must have been used for carriages in the old days. Twin iron gates had been pulled back to allow entry.

I turned slowly into the whitewashed tunnel and the exhaust of the Jaguar boomed in its confines. The tunnel opened into a cobbled mews that ran parallel to the avenue. There was another sign that directed me to turn left along the mews. I passed between the back of the hotel, scarred with black-painted fire escapes and water pipes, and the front of half a dozen bijou residences that had once been stables and were now *pied-à-terres* with brightly painted doors and shiny-leafed shrubs in tubs outside them.

I braked to a halt in front of a metal barrier that broke a link fence topped with razor wire. On the left of the barrier was a small, half-glassed booth. Inside was a black guy in a brown uniform complete with peaked cap. He was leaning against the back wall, looking bored. Outside stood two big white geezers in lounge suits. One held a clipboard. The one with the board said something to the other, who was carrying a portable phone, and walked through the narrow gap between the barrier and the fence and up to the driver's window of my car. I lowered the window all the way. There was a name tag clipped to the lapel of his suit. Under a multi-coloured logo that read 'Premiere Security' was typewritten 'Jack'.

'May I help you, sir?'

'I'm here to see Roger Lomax.'

'Your name, please?'

'Sharman. Nick Sharman.'

Jack consulted the clipboard 'Have you any ID, sir?'

I passed him my driver's licence and he read it without moving his lips and handed it back. He glanced down at the paper on his board and walked around the front of the car to check the registration.

'Fine, Mr Sharman,' he said. 'Drive straight in, across the courtyard and down the ramp. Park on the first level, please. Go through the fire door and someone will take you to Mr Lomax.'

'Thank you.'

He signalled to the black guy who pushed a button and the barrier lifted. I engaged low drive and the car bumped across the ramp between cobbles and concrete, slid smoothly across the courtyard, through an entrance two car widths wide, and into a sodium-lit tunnel that dropped sharply away in front of the bonnet of the car. The tunnel was neatly divided in two by a kerbstone set into the middle of the road. On my side, large white arrows pointed downwards; on the other side, the reverse. I let the Jaguar coast until the road levelled and a sign above me read: LEVEL ONE. I found an empty space and parked.

I switched off the engine and all I could hear was my own blood pounding through my head and the ticking of the engine as it began to cool. I opened the driver's door and stepped into chilly air that smelled of oil and petrol and cellulose. There was an orange EXIT sign above a grey-painted fire door about fifteen yards from where I'd stopped. I locked the door and dropped the keys into my pocket and looked at the six cars in the parking bays adjacent to mine. Six white Porsche 911 SE cabriolets, each one with a cream soft top. Beautiful. I figured there was close on half a million quid's worth of automobiles parked there. And the numberplates were PB 1 to 6 inclusive. Not a bad life, I thought, being a rock star. Mind you, I wouldn't have swapped any of them for my E-Type, old as it was.

As I stood there looking, the door under the sign burst open and two men and a woman came into the parking garage. One of the men was short, in his mid-forties, dressed in denim jeans and shirt, scuffed baseball boots, a down-filled waistcoat and a blue baseball cap, with NY printed on the front in yellow. Thin salt and pepper hair sprouted from under the cap, and down below his shoulders. The man with him wore a lounge suit like the guys on the gate. He looked like them too, but sans name plate. The woman was tall and blonde, about thirty and pretty good-looking under the artificial light. She was dressed in a short, spangled, red evening dress, even at that early hour. It was cut low at the back and front and exposed a mile of tanned flesh. The geezer in denim made straight for my car. 'Great motor,' he said. His accent was English tinged with American, just like Roger Lomax's. 'Want to sell it?'

'No.'

'Go on, you gotta. I'll give you twenty grand.'

'No.'

'What do you mean, no?' He sounded like someone who was used to having his every wish fulfilled. 'Thirty.'

'No,' I said again.

'Tell him, Pat,' the guy in denim said to his male companion.

His companion shrugged, and I almost heard his muscles creak. 'It's up to him,' he said. 'It's his car.'

'Fifty grand,' said the guy in denim.

That was so far over market value as to be a joke. 'No,' I said. 'And I'm late. Thanks for the offer.' I body swerved around the trio and made for the door. I pulled it open and two more huge geezers were standing in the tiny foyer. Again, both were wearing name tags. This time the portable phone was lying on a chair next to the lift door. The smaller of the two men held a clipboard. His tag read: 'Ronnie'.

'Sir?' he said.

'Nick Sharman to see Roger Lomax. I've an appointment with him at three.'

Ronnie didn't have to consult his clipboard. Apparently the word was out. 'Yes, Mr Sharman,' he said. 'Are you armed?'

'No,' I said back, and I wasn't.

'You won't mind if we check?'

I did, but I knew I wouldn't get past these two if I said no.

'OK,' I said. 'Go ahead.'

The bigger of the two, who was extremely big, believe me, and whose name tag read 'Big Phil' just to drive the point home, gave me a quick and thorough search. He shook his head at his partner. 'Thank you, Mr Sharman,' said Ronnie. 'My colleague will show you the way.'

So that's what they called them now.

Big Phil pressed the button to summon the lift and the door opened immediately. 'This way,' he said and ushered me inside. It had recently been swept and sprayed with perfume. It was a bit different to most car-park lifts. My guide pressed the button marked 1, and the lift sped upwards. He aimed his stare at a spot two feet below the top of the lift door and kept it there. I stood behind him and aimed my stare at the suppurating boil between his hair-line and his stiff white collar and kept it there. I can play tough too. We were both silent during the short journey.

A bell rang, and the lift doors opened on the first floor as bidden. Big Phil stood to one side to let me out first. I found myself in a vaulted hall tastefully furnished in what was supposed to be Chippendale but probably wasn't. The hall walls and ceiling were painted dusty pink and carpeted with a matching shag pile that was so thick it could have concealed a machine-gun nest. Big Phil walked me across the carpet to double doors with a discreet sign reading: BAR.

'Mr Lomax is waiting for you inside,' he said and pushed the doors open for me. I entered but he didn't follow. The room was in almost complete darkness. The only illumination was the oasis of light that was the bar itself. Behind it two barmen were conversing in muted tones, both polishing already gleaming glasses. Hidden speakers were playing Verdi at a volume so low as to be almost inaudible. I always reckon you get the muzak you pay for. I walked through the darkness and approached the bar. 'Mr Lomax?' I said with a question mark attached.

The taller of the barmen said, 'On the upper level, sir, in the first booth.' He pointed with one hand and I turned and allowed my eyes to get accustomed to the twilight and squinted in the direction he'd indicated. The bar area, which was huge and empty, was lined with screened-off booths. Tables and chairs were spaced across the floor just far enough apart for privacy. In the far corner of the room a pair of dark wood steps led to an area that resembled a large stage. At the back of the raised area were three more booths. The interior of the right-hand booth suddenly flared with light as whoever was sitting there struck a match and lit a cigarette. Roger Lomax I presumed and surfed across more shag pile, this time of a much darker shade, up the steps and across to the booth. I saw two dark eyes glitter in the reflection of the coal of the cigarette as they watched me approach.

'Roger Lomax?' I asked.

'Nick Sharman?'

'Yes.'

'Good afternoon, thanks for being so prompt. Come and join me.' Off the phone, his mid-Atlantic accent was more pronounced, and it grated on my ears.

I slid into the booth. It was pitch dark except for the firefly of red at the tip of his cigarette. He must have read my mind. 'Would you like a little light?' he asked.

'Why not?'

He turned and reached to the back of the booth and found a switch. A single dim bulb in a glass shade struggled to illuminate us. 'Is that better?'

'Yes,' I said.

He was sprawled across all three seats opposite me, with his back supported by the wall. The way he was sitting, I couldn't tell if he was tall or short. I guessed he was between thirty and thirty-five with real thick, real long, black hair that he kept pushing out of his face with big, strong-looking hands. On the third finger of his right hand was an extravagant silver and turquoise ring. Even in the faint light he looked tanned and fit. He was dressed in a black shirt and a black jacket that was patrolled with a design in jet beads that reflected the light. In front of him was a glass the size of a small soup tureen filled with a pale liquid, two packets of Marlboro Lite, a book of hotel matches, an ashtray and a shiny brown foolscap folder with the hotel name embossed in gold upon it. The ashtray was already full to overflowing.

'Would you like a drink?' he asked.

'Thanks.'

'What'll you have?'

I pointed at his glass. 'What's that?'

'Daiquiri.'

'That'll do.'

I didn't see the gesture but the barman did. He must have had eyes like a vulture. He appeared at the booth within seconds. 'Mr Lomax?'

'Two more of these,' said Roger Lomax, gesturing at his glass.

'And make a big jug. This could be a long afternoon.'

The barman exchanged the full ashtray for an empty one, nodded and left.

'Did you have any trouble getting in?'

'No, it was very efficient.'

'Good.'

'You have excellent security here.'

'After what happened to Trash, I thought we needed some.'

'Trash?' I asked.

'Danny. Danny Shapiro. We call him Trash. He used to collect garbage for the city in New York. Nearly everyone in the band and crew's got a nickname. It's a game we play. Anyway, after what happened I called up the firm that does our tour security in Europe. They rent out heavies by the yard.'

'They're very polite,' I said.

'They're paid to be. But they have another side to them.'

'I can imagine. Don't the other guests object?'

15

Roger Lomax smiled. 'There are no other guests. We've taken the entire hotel for two months.'

I can't say I wasn't impressed. 'You like a little elbow room then?'

'Not really. This is just a small place. There's only thirty-six apartments in the hotel, and twenty-five are being used by us right now. We always like a few spare for emergencies. We carry a large entourage of camp followers. We always stay here when we're in London. The management are very understanding and the staff discreet and obliging.'

As if to prove his point, the barman returned with two more huge glasses on a silver tray. He slid them in front of us and vanished without a word. 'I see what you mean,' I said.

'That's nothing, believe me.' I did, but didn't ask for details. 'This is a rock 'n' roll hotel,' he went on. 'An upmarket one, it's true, but rock 'n' roll through and through. It's owned by someone who understands the business, used to be in it. The manager doesn't have to justify his existence to a conglomerate. The people here are prepared to overlook a little high spirits, supply food and booze at all hours. The bars stay open until the last person leaves. They don't mind a few extra people staying over some nights. There's a tennis court, olympic-sized swimming pool, Nautilus gym, snooker and pool rooms in the basement. They'll even go so far as to redecorate if someone objects to the colour scheme in their suite. At a price, of course. A very high price. Refuse to pay and you'll never get a reservation again.'

'Everything costs.'

'This is true. So we can just come in here and pull up the drawbridge and party, you know what I mean?'

'Not really.'

'You will.'

'If I want to take the job.'

'Why shouldn't you?'

'Let me ask you a question first – what makes you think someone tried to murder your man? What exactly happened?'

'This is confidential, right?'

'Of course.'

'He took some bad cocaine.'

'Bad? How?' I asked.

'The worst way. It wasn't coke at all. It was smack. He OD'd.'

'Hmm.'

'Now you see what I mean about murder?'

I nodded. 'When did this all happen exactly?'

'Last night. Well, this morning to be precise. Three a.m. We got the hotel doctor. He got Trash to the Cromwell Hospital. They cleaned him out. It was a close call. He's still there, under guard. He'll be out in a couple of days and back to work.'

'Where did the stuff come from?'

'He doesn't know.'

'How come?'

'He's a coke freak. To the max. He's got Charlie stashed all over the shop. The guy would hide coke in his baby's diapers, if he had a baby.'

'Do you know who was here in the hotel when it happened?' I asked.

'I've got a guest and room list in here.' He tapped the brown folder in front of him.

'That's not what I asked,' I said. 'Do you know exactly who was in the hotel this morning? Who Shapiro was with? What everyone's movements were?'

'It's confused. There was a party going on.'

'Someone must know who was there.'

'People were coming and going. You know how it is.'

'Yeah, I know how it is. But what the hell do you want me to do?'

'Find out exactly what did happen.'

'An accident maybe?'

'Not the first.'

'No?'

'No. Some tapes got wiped in the studio. A lot of work went down the drain, and a lot of cash. And other things – small things, equipment going missing. Nothing much on its own but…'

'It could be coincidence.'

'It *could* be. Find out for me. Ask around.'

'Have you considered that people here might not want to help me? I've got no authority. Get the police in, it's not too late. They'll probably smack your wrist for being tardy, but so what? I'm sure you've had worse. People tend to answer their questions.'

'No police.'

'You keep saying that. Why not?'

'When I spoke to McBain about you, he said you weren't stupid.'

'I'm not.'

'Then join the dots. The last thing I want is the police poking around in here. This is a great big money factory. The band earn a lot, a fuck of a lot. We have less than a month to finish the new album. It's all scheduled. The record company reps have sold it into the shops. Ads have been booked in the trades. More importantly, the week it's due out is a very quiet one for releases. It's the optimum date for it to go to number one, worldwide, first week. Lots of editorial space has been earmarked for interviews. Christ, there's a six-month copy date on some of the glossies. The interviews are in, and I don't intend for them to come out and no new product in the stores. Two TV documentaries are scheduled for the week of release, one here, one in the States. The publicity machine has started to grind, and once started it's hard to stop. If we miss the date it won't be fatal, but we will lose maybe a couple of million unit sales worldwide. We don't *need* those sales but we sure want them.

'A month ago Keith Pandora's mother gets ill, very ill, maybe terminal. She can't be moved and he insisted on coming home. She's the only mother he's got and he wanted to be here, just in case. Now as it happens we're playing five nights at Wembley Arena two months from now.' He tapped the table top for emphasis. 'That's at the start of the World Tour that'll keep them on the road for months. Up to, including and long past the album release date. So you see time is tight. What we do is cancel our studio time in LA, buy time in London, which won't be easy at short notice, believe me, and book this place for two months. We've already got it reserved around the week we're at Wembley. In fact, it would be cheaper to buy the fucking place at the rates we're paying.' He shuddered at the thought.

'You have no idea what it's costing us to suspend work on the album.' He gave me a look of such pure sincerity as he spoke that he almost had me believing he gave a damn. Almost.

'I've hired a sound stage at Shepperton for live rehearsal, and brought over key road crew. I'll fly the rest over in time for the concerts and maybe pick up a few here. Representatives of the lawyers and accountants have come over with us and they're working from suites on the third floor. So what we've done in essence is move *Pandora's Box's* base of operations from Los Angeles to London.

'See, these people are different. I know them. I know their drinks and drugs of choice. Who they've fucked and who they'd like to fuck. I even know what make of tampons the girls favour. I should do, I've had to buy them enough times. This is our world. It's a closed world and we look after our own business. Clean business and dirty business. We get away with a lot. The punters expect it. What I don't need is a bunch of London cops tramping around in here. It upsets the creative flow.'

'So does murdering one of the band.'

'Exactly,' he said, without a trace of irony. 'We need someone who knows a little bit about the business.'

'I don't.'

'McBain says different. He says you're cool. I've known him a long time, and what he says goes with me. So will you take the job?'

I didn't answer. 'Attempted murder is serious,' I said.

'Look, Nick, I can't even be sure it *was* attempted murder. Maybe Trash did get things mixed up. It happens. But I swear to God I've never known him take horse. Maybe it was just someone's idea of a joke that went wrong. I just want a clue without calling in the law. We may be able to get away with a lot, but we're still vulnerable. Three of the band and most of the crew are American. I don't want anyone busted and deported. That would bring the album to a halt and my career with it. Do me a favour, Nick, say you'll help. Here's that list of everyone booked into the hotel. I've spoken to them and they're prepared to talk to you. Well, most are. They're pretty spooked about Trash, all of them, whatever front they put on.'

'He's that important?'

'At the moment, yes. You see there's only one track on the album left to do and it's written by him, sung by him, and all the guitar parts are his. The bass and drum tracks were laid down at the weekend. We need him for the lead guitar and vocal parts and time's getting short. And we can't go without him.'

'You have a month.'

'A month to finish one track is nothing for this lot. The album after *Regrets* took three years to record and that only had nine tracks on it. A month is fast work, believe me.'

He fell silent and so did I. I sipped my drink and lit a cigarette. 'So where exactly do you fit in?' I asked finally.

'I was wondering when you'd ask. I'm the man. I look after the money factory. I procure things and smooth the way, and when things go wrong I grease the palms so that things go right again.'

'Do they go wrong a lot? You seem to have all the bases covered.'

'Are you kidding? Just look at the mess we're in now. In this business, things always go wrong. It's the only constant you can count on. I've been in the industry for twenty years. I started as a gofer for Jack Barry at The Marquee. I did a couple of Reading festivals, then joined *Family* as a backline roadie.'

'What?'

'I looked after the onstage amps and stacks. I went to the States with them twice, and stayed. I worked for Capitol Records as a plugger. What I was really doing was supplying cash and coke to the FM stations on the West Coast. Then I joined Atlantic, did the same. Then I got promoted to special projects.'

I looked at him.

'Don't ask,' he said. 'I did one tour with *Zeppelin* before Bonzo died, then tour-managed Elton John, and when he stopped touring in eighty-one I hitched up with *The Box*. I've been with them ever since.'

'You come from London?'

'Originally. East End through and through… at least, I was. I went back for the first time in years a couple of weeks ago. Shit, man, they've ruined that part of town. It was never all that great, but now …'

'Times change,' I said. 'And governments. Anyway I thought you'd have been a Tory, with all this.' I gestured round the bar.

'American citizen now. Straight Democrat ticket. That's another reason I don't want any deportations. I might be first.'

'It sounds like you have a good life.'

'It is. I'm very well paid. Very. And I have an expense account that means I never have to touch my salary. I have absolute control over a bank account that contains enough funds to make your eyes water. I carry every major credit card, all the bills are covered, and I don't have to supply receipts. I have an apartment in Beverly Hills and shop on Rodeo Drive. I have a very beautiful woman who lives in that apartment whom I haven't seen for months and might not see again for another six, or maybe longer. She's probably balling the world. I know I am. I have the choice of eighteen cars. I travel first class. Soon, I'm sure, my shit won't stink. For a boy from Plaistow, who never lived in a house with an inside toilet until he was fifteen, I reckon that's not bad.'

'Not bad at all, so why are you so pissed off?'

'Sorry, Nick. Sometimes I ramble. Too many of these.' He tapped his glass.

'Me too,' I said. And it was true.

'So listen, I've got a suite for you,' he said. 'It's very pleasant, second floor, on the corner with a view of the square.'

'Do you think I'll approve of the colour scheme?'

'I hope so. Does that mean you'll take the job?'

'I don't know.'

Just then the door of the bar opened and a woman came into the room. She walked over to the bar and said something to the barmen. One reached down and touched a switch, and recessed lights in the ceiling and walls winked on. It wasn't the Blackpool illuminations but at least you could see to count the fingers on your hand.

I looked over at Lomax. 'Isn't that Ninotchka?'

He nodded. 'None other.'

I checked the woman out. She didn't look much from a distance, but she was a bona fide, 22-carat rock star with a capital R and a capital S. Apart from the success she'd had with *Pandora's Box* she'd released several solo albums which had charted, and had three top ten singles in her own right. She'd been in two movies, one Oscar-nominated, and had by all accounts fucked enough famous geezers to qualify for a double-page spread in the *Guinness Book of Records*.

The barman mixed her a drink, and when he passed her the glass she made towards us. She was wearing a chamois leather suit with a short jacket and a long, full skirt that revealed a hint of white petticoat at the hem. The jacket was unbuttoned over a silk camisole top with lots of lace detail, and by the way her nipples poked through the thin material, and jiggled as she walked like two tiny loaded pistols, nothing underneath. Her high-heeled, lace-up boots matched the colour of her suit to perfection. She was wearing a lot of tom. About fifty narrow silver bracelets on each wrist, silver rings on every finger including a twin of the one Roger Lomax wore. Around her neck was a silver and turquoise necklace and in one ear was an extravagant earring of silver and bright blue feathers, more than six inches long. Her hair was dusty blonde, and tied back so that just a few wisps hung around her ears. She was tanned golden, and the shade of lipstick she wore set off the tan to perfection.

'Do you always have to sit in the dark, Roger?' she asked. 'I swear you were a vampire in a previous life.' She had a real American accent and played it to the gallery, which was me.

'Ninotchka, this is Nick Sharman,' said Roger Lomax. 'He's an old friend of Mark McBain's.'

'Wow, how did you manage that? McBain's as hard to tie down as smoke,' she said, generating about ten thousand watts of pure California girlism.

'I managed,' I said, and offered her my hand.

Her jewellery rattled as she took it. Her grip was strong and dry.

'Nick Sharman, this is Ninotchka,' Roger Lomax finished the introduction.

What do you say? I've seen your tits in *Playboy*. I've seen you all sweated up, frolicking with some butch geezer in your last video. I saw your arse in the movie when you were supposed to be screwing Jack Nicholson. I said none of those things. 'How do you do?' was all I said.

'You Englishmen are so polite,' she said back. 'At first.' And gave

Roger a dirty look. I sensed there was unfinished business there, and I didn't want to know about it.

Up close, and even in the half-light of the bar, Ninotchka was showing signs of wear and tear around the edges. Hard boozing wear and tear, hard living wear and tear. But on her it looked good. Besides, she looked as if she could care less.

She sat down and helped herself to one of Lomax's cigarettes. 'What do you do, Nick?' she asked.

'He's a private cop,' Lomax answered for me. 'I've asked him to find out who spiked Trash.'

'You don't look much like Dick Tracy.'

'I'm not,' I said modestly.

'You going to ask me some questions?'

'Maybe. I haven't made up my mind whether to take the job or not.' But I was beginning to.

'Wanna take me to dinner tonight?' she asked.

That sort of offer you don't get from that sort of woman twice in a lifetime. 'Yeah, sure,' I said, almost tripping over my tongue.

'I'm in the Mayfair Suite. Corny but true. Pick me up at seven. I get too hungry for dinner at eight.' And she started half singing, half humming *The Lady is a Tramp* as she finished her drink, stood up and left us.

I looked at Lomax and he looked back at me and I don't think he liked what he saw. 'Seems like you've taken the job then?'

'Seems like it.'

'I'd be very careful there if I were you, Nick. You're just her type, I know it. I'll tell you exactly what's going to happen. She'll give you her full attention, ignore everyone else. She'll only speak through you. She'll ask your advice on everything, and take it. You'll choose her clothes and her next single. She'll buy you the complete Gaultier summer collection. You'll be walking around three feet off the ground. Then she'll cut you off at the knees, brother. She'll chop off your dick, spread it with mustard, put it in a roll and gobble it up. You'll be castrated, and you'll probably hand her the scalpel, you'll love her so much.'

'Sounds like the voice of experience.'

'You'd better believe it! I told you, I know what tampons she prefers. I'm giving you the good word, Nick. Just like I wish someone had done to me.'

'I'll bear it in mind.'

'No, you won't.'

He was wrong. I would. I was too old and ugly to fall into that kind of trap, or so I thought. 'If I'm going to stay here I'll need to go back and get some things,' I said, ignoring his comment.

'No need. I've taken care of everything. There's a good men's store in the foyer here. They'll fix you up with anything you need. I've taken the liberty of opening an account in your name.'

That was the sort of liberty I could handle.

'The band'll take care of the bill,' he went on.

Better and better, I thought.

'There's shaving gear and all that sort of stuff in your suite. *Anything* else you need, just call reception.'

'OK,' I said. 'You've sold me.' Although it wasn't really him who'd done it.

'So that just leaves the question of your fee? McBain wasn't very precise.'

'I don't think McBain ever paid me,' I said dryly.

'*We* pay. What do you charge?'

'Two hundred a day.' From the look on his face it was what he was used to paying for manicures.

He took a company-sized chequebook and pen from the inside pocket of his jacket. He wrote out a cheque and signed it with a flourish. He pushed it over and I looked at it. It was for fourteen hundred pounds.

'A week in advance,' he said. Even I could just about work that out. 'I don't know how long this sort of thing usually takes.'

'Me neither.'

'When you need more, let me know.'

'I will,' I said, and folded the cheque and put it in my shirt pocket. 'Well, now I'm weighed in you'd better tell me something about the band.'

'Like what?'

'Like who they are.'

'Don't you know?' He sounded amazed.

'Not really. I mean, I know about them, and the album, and I've heard loads of their songs on the radio. But they're not really my style. A bit too MOR, if you know what I mean.'

'I know *exactly* what you mean,' he said.

'And apart from Ninotchka, I wouldn't recognise one of them on the street.'

He shook his head in wonderment. 'Just as well I put the latest set of biogs in here then,' he said, and tapped the folder.

'You tell me about them,' I said. 'I can buy a magazine if I want to read what the PR people want me to read.'

'Right. I'll give you the basics now. More when you need it, OK?'

I nodded.

'Ninotchka you've met. She's on lead vocals. Writes a lot of songs. A lot of hits. Plays guitar. Not very well.'

Bitchy, I thought.

'We were an item. You're bound to find out. She was also an item with Pandora for a while, and a couple of guys that have since left. And several soundmen, roadies, lighting technicians, and even a couple of T-shirt salesmen.' You could tell he liked telling me that. 'Then there's Pandora himself. He's English. Formed the band with Tony Box in sixty-eight. There's been a lot of water under the bridge since then. He's on keyboards and vocals. He's been married, oh, four times at least. You tend to lose count. At the moment he's between marriages. Next Tony Box, the only other original member. He's English too. Plays lead. He's been married twice. His second wife's here now. Her name's Barby – you'd never guess. Trash is second lead guitar. He's a writer and singer. Brilliant. Don't know what they'd do without him. Baby Boy Valin – he's a drummer, what more can I say? Fucking nutter. Comes from LA. Been in a thousand bands. Shorty Long is on base. Nice guy. Scratch is on vocals, and she fiddles around with percussion. She's English too, but joined about seventy-one or -two. Used to be married to Keith.'

'Sounds interesting.'

'It can be. Sometimes we have to put barbed wire across the stage to keep these fuckers from killing each other.'

He stopped when he realised what he'd said.

'Freudian slip,' I said.

He didn't reply. 'And finally there's two back-up singers. There should be another one really to make up the full three stooges, but they do pretty well. Officially they're called *The Twilights*. Unofficially, the band bikes. So that's it, really. You'll meet them all as we go along. In fact, here's one now.'

I looked up as the door of the bar opened and a tall, thin man with long, curly hair came in accompanied by two young girls – very young. They were both real skinny with tiny breasts and similar heart-shaped faces. Although one was blonde and the other had black hair they were obviously sisters. They wore matching black mini-dresses, dark tights and high-heeled black shoes. They were both heavily made-up, but that seemed to accentuate rather than hide the immaturity in their faces.

'Which one's he?'

'Don't you recognise him? That's Keith Pandora. The Main Man. The Tsar.'

'Why do you call him that?'

'Because he runs the band like it was Imperial Russia.'

'Are those his kids?'

'Don't let him hear you say that, for Christ's sake! He's screwing them.'

'But they're only babies.'

'Don't you believe it. Their bodies may be young, but in their heads they're a thousand years old.'

'How old exactly?'

'The blonde's fourteen, the brunette, thirteen.'

'And he's fucking them?'

'Does it offend you?'

'I've got a daughter myself, not much younger than those two. If he touched her, I'd break his skinny neck.'

'OK, Nick, I read you. But can you cool it around Keith?'

I said nothing.

'Their mother's here with them if it makes you feel any better.'

'Not much.'

'They've got a suite close to yours.'

'What kind of mother is she, for fuck's sake?'

'An old groupie. She reckons one of the kids is Keith Moon's, the other's Iggy Pop's.'

'Terrific.'

Keith Pandora sat the two girls down at a table and came over to our booth. 'Hi, Keith,' said Roger Lomax.

'Hi,' said Pandora, looking at me.

'This is Nick Sharman.'

'I've heard about you,' said Pandora. 'Welcome aboard.' I nodded.

Up close he looked his age. His hair was still thick but his face was deeply lined and tired-looking under its tan. He was handsome in a self-indulgent way, with full, pouty lips and a large, hooked nose. He was dressed in what I imagined was rock-star chic: a black leather biker's jacket, a size too small, over a satin cowboy shirt with white piping and silver arrowheads on the points of the collars. Tight, faded jeans and black boots. 'Is Dodge looking after you?' he asked.

'Dodge?'

'Roger the Dodger,' said Pandora, and smiled showing yellow teeth. 'The best in the biz. Ain't that right, Dodge?'

'So they say.'

'I'll tell you how he got the name one day, Nick,' said Pandora. 'Right now I'm busy.' He grinned, and I thought how satisfying it would be to punch him in the mouth and mash his fat lips on to his big teeth.

'I'll look forward to it,' I said, and didn't know if I meant the story or the punch.

'See you later then.' And Pandora turned on a cowboy-booted heel and left.

'You shouldn't show your enthusiasm so much,' said Lomax. 'You almost bowled him over.'

'I'm working for the band, I don't have to like them,' I said. 'Get that straight now.'

He raised his hands in surrender. 'OK, OK, I gotcha.' Just then the door burst open and the short guy in denim I'd met in the garage entered with his little gang. They made for the booth where Lomax and I were sitting. The guy in denim half fell across the table and said to Roger, 'Hello, Dodge, going into town tonight?'

'No,' said Lomax. 'I'm staying here.'

The guy in denim slid into the booth next to me. 'Hello,' he said pleasantly. 'Who are you? Do you work here?'

I looked at Lomax. 'No,' he said. 'This is Nick Sharman. He's a detective, private. He's looking into our trouble.'

'Is that so?' said the guy in denim.

'Nick, this is Tony Box, his wife, Barby.' The woman in the red spangled dress smiled a greeting. 'And Pat, who drives them round, and generally takes care of business.' The big geezer nodded to me.

'We've met.'

'No,' said Box.

'In the garage. You tried to buy my car.'

Tony Box looked askance. 'No,' he said again. 'Did I? Did you sell it to me?'

'No.' It was my turn.

'Good. I've got enough cars as it is, and I've got no dough. Get us a drink, Dodge.'

Lomax did another of his invisible signals and beamed the barman in. 'What?' he asked.

'Jack Daniel's,' said Tony Box. 'A bottle for me, large brandy for the wife, Perrier for the driver, and whatever you two are having.' He sat next to me and breathed whisky into my face. If I'd had a match handy I could have set fire to his breath.

'What is it?' he asked me.

'What?'

'Your car.'

'Seventy-two E-Type, V-twelve hard top.'

'Nice car. Maybe I'll buy it after all.'

'Fine,' I said.

I looked over at Roger Lomax. He spoke to me as if Tony Box wasn't in the same room. I was beginning to wonder if he was from the same galaxy. 'He forgets everything,' he said softly. 'Except his lead lines and the number of his bank account.'

This guy was reaching levels of cynicism that even I would have had trouble scaling. Tony Box and his party hadn't heard a word of it.

Lomax shrugged and grinned, and his teeth reflected the light. He excused himself to Tony Box's wife like a perfect gentleman. 'I'll see you later, Nick, I know you won't be lonely,' he said. 'I've got my rounds to do.' And he walked across the carpet as if the strongest drink he'd had all day was semi-skimmed chocolate milk.

When he stood I saw that he was over six foot tall. He made a Machiavellian figure as he went across the room checking on each table as he went.

Roger the Dodger. I was beginning to see where he'd got his nick-name.

I'd have to watch him.

3

I sat and half listened to the other three in the booth chatting away, and watched Lomax go over to Keith Pandora's table and sit down. I guessed they were discussing me from the looks turned in my direction by the two men. The girls were deep in conversation with each other and ignoring the world.

The door to the bar kept opening and more people came in. There were all sorts of young, and young–middle-aged men and women coming into the bar. One particular crew caught my eye. There were three of them, all in their mid- to late-twenties. Two were huge, one much slimmer and smaller. They all wore identical silk jackets over clean denims teamed with fancy cowboy boots with underslung heels and long pointy toes. The jackets were bright purple with white sleeves. On the back of each was embroidered *Pandora's Box* in black script outlined in white. They had to be part of the road crew. The two big guys reminded me of someone I had once known.

All three were conversing loudly in American accents as they came in. They stopped and said hello to Lomax and Pandora and ignored the girls. They all squinted my way and the two big guys went to the bar whilst the smaller one made for the booth where I was. 'Hi, Tony,' said the roadie to Box. 'Hi, Princess,' to Box's wife. 'Pat,' to the driver.

'Hello, me old mate,' said Tony Box, looking a little bewildered as if he'd never seen him before. I was getting severely concerned for the guy's brain-cell count. He poured another half a tumbler of JD and took a long swallow as if he didn't have a care in the world. The other two just nodded. Nobody introduced me. 'You the cop?' the roadie said to me.

I nodded.

'Come and have a drink.'

Just then Lomax appeared at his shoulder. 'Later, Chippy,' he said. 'I'm getting him fixed up with a room.'

'Raincheck,' said the guy named Chippy to me.

'Sure,' I said. 'I'll look forward to it.'

Lomax took a key on a ring out of his pocket. 'Here's your key. I'll show you the way.'

I excused myself to Tony Box and said goodbye to his wife and Pat, and followed Lomax out of the bar. I gave Pandora and his girlfriends a long look as I went past. Only the blonde responded. She stuck out her tongue.

We stopped outside. 'Don't pay any attention to Tony,' said Lomax. 'He doesn't mean any harm. He's always stoned, that's all.'

'What on?' I asked.

'Not smack if that's what you're thinking. Dope. He smokes joints like cigarettes. It's done his brain in. He's cool. Quite funny, really, when he gets going.'

'I believe you.'

'Come on. It's only one floor. Let's walk,' said Lomax.

We went up a wide staircase lined with oil paintings, along a corridor, around a couple of corners, and Lomax stopped outside a door. A small brass plaque on the door read 'Sussex Suite'. 'It's not bad,' he said. 'Small but comfortable.' He gave me the key. 'Help yourself. I'll talk to you later.'

'Fine,' I said. 'See you soon.'

He left me on the threshold of the room and walked back down the corridor and out of sight around the corner. I let myself in. Comfortable it was, but small? You could easily have fitted my flat inside twice over.

The sitting room was comfortably furnished with a grey three-piece suite and a dining table with four upright chairs. On the table was a huge basket of fresh fruit. There was a big-screen TV with full satellite, video and two blue-film channels. In one corner was a bar complete with tiny sink, fridge and ice-making machine. The machine was full of fresh ice. Whisky, vodka, white rum, gin and brandy on optic, a freezer full of beer, a shelf full of more esoteric spirits and enough mixers to make a cocktail waiter green with envy. There was even a Jones' book of cocktail recipes. To the side of the bar was a small kitchen with sink, microwave, fridge and hob in case some rock star or other decided to make a bedtime cup of cocoa after a hard day at the recording studio. The fridge contained a dozen bottles of premium champagne.

I went back into the sitting room and through the connecting door to the bedroom. The bed was huge, with built-in bedside shelves and a control panel on both sides. The mattress was covered in a silk throw. The only other furniture was a large dressing table and stool. One wall was made of doors. I tried them. One was the door to the bathroom. Inside the others was a built-in wardrobe with shelves and drawers and full-length mirrors in the doors. I closed the doors and sat on the bed. I looked at the control panel. I pressed one button and the radio came on, another and a TV set rose out of the floor at the foot of the bed. Another and the ceiling above the bed rolled away to reveal a huge mirror. I got the ceiling back and didn't try any of the other buttons.

I went into the bathroom. Lomax had been right about the shaving kit. The bathroom was fully stocked in all departments. There was a nine-foot diameter circular, sunken bath with Jacuzzi. A shower stall big enough to fit a five-a-side football team, with a shower head the size of a cauliflower. The toilet had a mahogany seat with a small "Jones" discreetly carved at the back and picked out in gold leaf. On the wall over the hand basin was a mirrored cabinet. Inside was a gold-plated safety razor and a packet each of Wilkinson and Gillette double-edged blades, shaving foam for every skin type, a block of solid shaving soap in a glass jar, and a badger-hair shaving brush monogrammed with the name of a Jermyn Street barber. There were four different kinds of toilet soap, a boxed set of hair-brush and comb, a packet of condoms and a box of sanitary towels. Something for everyone.

On a hook behind the door hung two XL, thick white towelling robes with "Jones" picked out in red stitching on the breast. I went through the bedroom and opened one of the wardrobe doors with a mirror and took a squint at myself. I felt that I could get away with the dark suit I'd been wearing all day on my dinner date, but I fancied a clean shirt. I went into the sitting room.

There was a hotel directory next to the phone. I flicked through it and found the number for the Men's Shoppe. Shoppe, how quaint, I thought, and hoped that the clobber was better than the name. I dialled though. 'Men's shop,' said a voice. At least he hadn't pronounced it 'Shoppy'.

'Hello,' I said. 'This is Nick Sharman in the Sussex Suite.'

'How can I help you, Mr Sharman?'

'Roger Lomax told me I could get a shirt from you.'

'Of course.'

I told him I wanted a white shirt, and my size.

'Anything else, sir?'

'Perhaps some socks, black.' I told him my shoe size.

'No problem,' said the voice. 'I'll get them up to you directly.'

'Thank you.'

'Our pleasure. Goodbye, Mr Sharman.'

I went over to the bar and made a weak vodka and tonic. Five minutes later there was a tap on the outside door. 'Come in,' I said.

The door opened and a very spruce young man in a navy blue suit entered. Behind him were two more young guys carrying a pile of clothes each. 'Mr Sharman,' said the one in the blue suit, 'I'm Jeremy. I run the shop downstairs.' The two other guys started laying clothes over the sofa and the armchairs. 'You ordered a shirt.'

'Yes,' I said. 'Just a shirt and some socks.'

'I thought I'd bring you up some samples of our other merchandise. Firstly, of course, there are some shirts. I brought a couple of white ones and some alternative shades, maybe not *quite* so severe. There are half a dozen pairs of socks too. But I thought you might like to try on a jacket or two. Then there are some trousers, a few ties and a suit.

Plus, of course, some shoes. Mr Lomax told me you have nothing with you. I also brought some underwear. I guessed your sizes from what you told me on the phone.' He looked me over. 'I think I was about right, but I can do alterations within the hour so there's no problem. I'll leave them with you. Please try them on at your own convenience. Naturally anything you don't want I'll take back.' He stood, arms folded, with one finger under his chin. 'But I don't think I was wrong.'

I was quite taken aback. 'Do you want me to sign anything?'

'Oh no, Mr Sharman. Don't sign until you're satisfied you want the clothes. If you could stop by sometime and let me know what you want to keep, I'll arrange for the rest to be collected.'

'That's very good of you,' I said. 'I appreciate it.'

'Nothing's too good for our guests.'

The three excused themselves and left. I took a closer look at the booty strewn across the room.

There were three jackets. The names on the labels inside were so close to the cutting edge of male high fashion as almost to be a danger to themselves. Nothing was priced. I took them into the bedroom and tried them on in front of a mirror. They fitted perfectly. I figured, what the hell? and tried on the trousers and the suit and a couple of shirts. I was like a kid let loose in a toyshop. I thought a pair of off-white cuffed strides teamed with a dark blue, double-breasted jacket with a paisley lining over a pale blue button-down shirt and patterned tie looked pretty good. I finished the outfit off with a pair of navy blue, thick-soled, American loafers I found in a box. I hung the rest of the clothes in the wardrobe, draped the jacket over the sofa, made another vodka tonic and turned on the TV. I sat in one of the armchairs and lit a cigarette and looked through the list of hotel guests Lomax had supplied. Frankly it got me nowhere, and I started watching a Robert Mitchum film. He was playing a private eye in Chicago in the fifties. It was deeply noir and I was getting well into it when the telephone rang.

I cut the sound on the TV with the remote and picked up the receiver. It was Lomax. 'What's up?' I asked.

'Nothing. Just checking that you were settled in OK.'

'I am,' I said. 'Nice place. Don't bother with the decorators, I like it as it is.'

'Good.'

'I got some new clothes.'

'I told Jeremy to look after you.'

'He did.'

'Good, what's next?'

'Dinner with Ninotchka.'

'I meant about Trash.'

'I'll need to talk to him.'

'When?'

'Tomorrow?'

'Fine, I'll fix it.'

'I'd like to speak to anyone who was with him that evening, and the rest of the band too.'

'I'll speak to Trash's wife. She'll know who was around that night. The rest of the band are free at the moment.'

'I'll start with Ninotchka tonight and slot some more in tomorrow.'

'I warn you, Nin and Trash don't get on, so don't pay too much attention to what she says. As for the rest of the band, just let me know when you want to see them. You have carte blanche around here.'

'I'm flattered.'

'Don't be, just get the truth.'

'I'll try,' I said.

'Enjoy your evening.'

'I'm sure I will.'

'*I'm* sure you will. Just one other thing.'

'What?'

'Someone else wants to see you.'

'Who?'

'Guy called Pascall. Corporate lawyer. One of the guys I told you about who came in from LA. Big deal, or at least he thinks so. He's in the Surrey Suite. Can you go up and see him?'

'When?'

'Now.'

I looked at my watch. 5.45. 'Sure.'

'And be nice. What he thinks matters, unfortunately.'

'I'll be on my best behaviour, I promise.'

'I wouldn't expect anything less. See you.' And he hung up.

4

I put down the phone, put on my jacket and went calling on the big-deal lawyer. I knocked on the door of the Surrey Suite at 5.55 precisely.

'Come,' said a voice. It was the second best offer I'd had all day, so I did.

I opened the door and went in. The room was dark, except for one spot lamp in the far corner behind a high-backed chair, lit and angled to throw it into silhouette. In the chair, almost invisible, sat someone.

So this is the bloody lawyer, I thought. If he was into ego trips, no wonder the real stars were such painful fuckers. I walked across the room towards him, hoping that he hadn't placed anything in the way as a booby trap.

'Mr Sharman, welcome,' said a disembodied American voice as I got closer. That was reassuring. At least I knew I was in the right place. 'Do sit down.' There was a low chair on my side of him. It was perfectly placed so that whoever sat there had to look up at the speaker, and sit with the spot right in their eyes. This guy had obviously done some research into behavioural psychology.

I moved the chair slightly and sat down. So had I. If he'd been that good he'd've had the chair nailed to the floor. He made no comment, just said, 'You may smoke if you wish.'

I took out a cigarette. There was an ashtray on the arm of the chair.

'My name is Pascall,' he said. 'Louis Pascall. I am a partner in the company that handles the legal affairs of *Pandora's Box*. When I heard what had happened to Danny, naturally I came straight here. I told Roger I wanted no police involvement. I also told him to use his best endeavours to protect the band. He hired extra men from Premiere, and you.' He didn't exactly sound thrilled skinny about that. 'Naturally, I asked him why.'

'Naturally,' I said.

'He mentioned that you had done a job for Mark McBain.'

I nodded.

'I made further enquiries and the name Salvatore Cassini was mentioned.'

Salvatore Cassini, Jo's father. The name swept over me like a black wave. Josephine Cassini. Little Jo. The woman I'd loved and lost in a car-bomb explosion meant for me. It all happened because I was looking into the financial affairs of Mark McBain, rock star. A victim of the sixties. Ripped off by his management company and living the life of a virtual recluse in a huge house in Surrey.

But the people who'd planted the bomb had picked on the wrong woman to kill. Her father was a very heavy-duty Family man, with a capital 'F'. And in more ways than one, if you catch my drift. Cassini had sent his only son and a couple of soldiers to sort out the bombers. But things had gone badly wrong for all of us, and everyone involved had died except for McBain and me.

'I'm familiar with the name,' I said.

'Do you know him personally?' Pascall asked.

'No,' I said. 'You?'

'We've never met, but the family still has outstanding connections. An acquaintance of mine filled me in on the whole story. Apparently a lot of good men died that day.'

'And a lot of bad ones.'

'Salvatore Cassini has never left the house since his son and daughter died.'

'He's retired?' I asked.

'Not exactly. His tentacles still reach far. They have a million tiny suckers.'

Suckers is right, I thought.

'Are you part of the Mob?' I asked.

'Mr Sharman, really. No one calls them that these days.'

'Slap my wrist,' I said. 'Are you?'

'No. But…'

'But the record business is full of them. Right?'

'Right.'

'Is that what all this is about?'

'No.'

'You know them, but they're not involved?'

'Take my word for it. I've made other enquiries. Whatever this is, it's not that.'

'Well, I'll have to find out exactly what it is then.'

'That is why we're paying you.'

'Your man Shapiro insists he doesn't know where the drugs came from,' I said.

'Do you believe him?'

'I haven't spoken to him yet. I'll tell you when I do.'

'And when will that be?'

'Tomorrow morning.'

'Fine.' I felt I was being dismissed. Then he said, 'Mr Sharman, before you go – I judge by results. That's all. Give me results and you'll have my backing one hundred per cent. And my gratitude. That comes in many forms. Otherwise…,' He didn't finish.

I couldn't believe it. The guy was actually sitting there in the middle of this stage-managed bullshit and threatening me, as if I was the one putting the bite on him. What a piece of sleaze, I thought. 'Listen, Mr Pascall,' I said, 'I took this job for one reason and one reason only: because I was asked out to dinner by a woman who most men would crawl across broken glass to hear piss in a tin cup – over the phone. I didn't do it for the money or your gratitude. As far as I'm concerned, with your gratitude and a quid I can get a cup of coffee. Don't even think of threatening me. I've had it done by experts. If I don't like what I see, colour me out of here. Do I make myself clear?'

He didn't answer. All he said was, 'Ninotchka.'

'The one and only,' I said.

'And you're the latest?'

'We're going out to dinner, that's all.'

'That's what they all say, Mr Sharman. She's never been sparing with her favours. The woman must have an iron lining in her cunt. A gynaecological miracle.'

I didn't even bother to answer. Just left his words hanging in the air. I think he got the point, or maybe he was too insensitive. Like I said, a piece of sleaze.

'So, Mr Sharman, I'll leave you to your investigation,' he said. 'You will make regular reports?'

'Of course.'

'Then you can go.'

'I wouldn't have dared, without your permission,' I said, and left.

When I got outside, it occurred to me that I could have handled it better.

I went back to my suite and made a fresh drink. By the time I'd finished it, it was time to call on Ninotchka in the Mayfair Suite.

5

It was on the top floor on the farthest corner from mine. I tapped politely on the door at five to seven. A heavyweight from the security firm opened the door. His name tag read 'Don'.

'Yes?' he said.

'I'm here to see Ninotchka.'

'And you are?'

'Nick Sharman.'

'Come in.'

I stepped through the door and into a hippy dream. The sitting room was twice as big as mine. The curtains were drawn and the lights dim. Where possible they'd been draped in gypsy scarves to diffuse them even further. The carpet had been covered with overlapping oriental rugs and brightly coloured cushions had been scattered over two big sofas and three armchairs. Joss sticks were burning in holders and the room was rich with the smell. The room had been personalised further with a big CD player, amp and speakers. It was playing muted rock. I recognised a track from *Exile on Main Street*. The room had three other doors. Don went over and tapped on one. I heard a woman's voice reply, and he opened the door, entered and closed it behind him. A moment later he re-appeared. 'Come through, Mr Sharman,' he said, and the tone of his voice was a little warmer, but not much.

I walked across the rugs and through the door. Inside was part office, part dressing room, with clothes on rails and hanging from anywhere that would hold them. There was a desk in the centre of the room holding a bunch of papers, two telephones and a fax machine. Two office chairs were drawn up to the desk. Ninotchka was sitting on one speaking on the phone. 'My date's here, must go, Mom. Call you tomorrow. Love you – 'bye,' she said and hung up. She spun round on the chair and looked at me. 'Hi, Nick. How are you?'

'Just fine.'

She looked me over. 'Did you get that jacket downstairs?'

'Yes.'

'Roger's got one exactly the same. The trouble with shopping in hotels is that sooner or later everyone gets to dress exactly the same.'

'I thought it looked pretty good.'

'Hey, it looks fine, it's just…'

'What?'

'You look like a second-string record producer or the manager of a Mid-West heavy metal band that's just broken the top forty.'

'Is that bad?'

'Not at all, but you could look like the president of Columbia Records if you tried.'

'Is that good?'

She ignored the question and jumped up. 'What do you think of this?' she demanded, and did a twirl in front of me. She was wearing a simple cotton jersey dress, hooped in blue and white, with a short skirt. It clung so close that I guessed she was wearing very little else. She looked great.

'Great,' I said.

'That's what I want to say when I see you. "Great", nothing else.'

'Do you want me to go and change?' I asked, perhaps a little tetchily.

She came over, reached up and kissed me full on the lips. 'Don't get mad,' she said. 'You look good. I can just see more potential, you know what I mean? I didn't say it to hurt you. Do you forgive me?'

What could I say? Her perfume was light and spacey and I liked it a lot. 'Sure.'

'I tell you what, I found a great shop the other day opposite Harrods. I've been dying to find a man to try it out. We'll go shopping tomorrow afternoon. How does that suit you?'

'I don't think…'

'Don't argue. I love buying presents. You'll upset me if you don't let me get you something.'

'I'm supposed to be working.'

'You will be working, looking after me.'

'Well…' I said.

'Say you will.'

What the hell? 'OK.'

'Great. Where shall we eat tonight?'

I shrugged.

'What's your favourite food?'

'Thai, Chinese, Indonesian.'

'Do you like Korean?'

'I don't know, I never tried it.'

'You'll love it. I'll get my jacket.' She went out of the room and I followed. She crossed to one of the other inside doors and went through. I waited in the sitting room with Don. He didn't speak. Nor did I.

She was back within a few seconds carrying a white jacket and a blue handbag that matched her dress. 'Night off, Don,' she said.

He looked from her to me. 'No, miss, I'm supposed to stay with you.'

'I have someone. He'll see me home, won't you, Nick?'

'Of course.'

'I dunno, miss.'

'Mr Sharman is very fierce. He'll keep the wolves at bay.'

Don looked at me and pulled a face. It wasn't my night for compliments for sure. 'I think I can manage,' I said.

'Chas will be driving,' said Ninotchka.

'I shouldn't,' said Don.

Ninotchka switched on the charm, full blast. 'I'll be all right, I promise.'

'I don't know what Mr Lomax will say.'

'You leave Mr Lomax to me.'

'OK, miss, but…'

'No buts, you go on home.'

'I'm on 'til one. I'll wait until then.'

'If you want, but I doubt that we'll be back.' I could see I was in for a long night.

'I'll wait, miss.'

'All right, Don. Help yourself to what you want. Have dinner.'

'Thanks, miss.'

'It's nothing. Coming, Nick?'

I nodded. I felt like the dog.

We went down to the foyer by lift. It was a much grander affair than the one from the car park, with a uniformed attendant, one of those old-fashioned wheels to operate it, and enough gilt inside the car to sink a ship.

As we entered the foyer a middle-aged man in a grey suit and holding a grey peaked cap jumped up from where he was sitting and made a bee-line for us. 'The car's outside, Miss Ninotchka. Where are we off to tonight?'

'All over,' she replied. 'I feel in a party mood. Meet Nick, he's looking after me tonight.'

'No Don?' asked Chas.

'No. I've given him a holiday.'

Then it was Chas's turn to give me a good screw. This little firm certainly took their responsibilities seriously. He seemed to find me a little more reassuring than Don had. 'All right, Miss Ninotchka, just as you like.'

I trailed after them outside to the black stretch limo that sat at the kerb. Chas smartly opened the rear door, and I followed Ninotchka into the back of the car. Chas got behind the wheel and Ninotchka touched a button that rolled down the glass divider between the driver's cab and the passenger compartment.

'Remember that restaurant we went to the other night?'

'Which one?'

'The Korean.'

'Sure.'

'Let's go.'

Chas started the car, put it into gear and pulled slowly away. Ninotchka let the divider roll up again. She smiled at me and dipped her hand into her bag and came out with a DAT cassette. 'I've just got the final mix of one of my songs on the album. Wanna hear it?'

'Sure.'

She slid the tape into the player mounted in the bulk-head of the car. 'It's an old Marc Bolan song,' she said. 'See if you recognise it.'

The speakers clicked and the song started. I recognised it. It wasn't one of his best, but it was good. Ninotchka's voice was well up in the mix, there was a manic guitar break, and a steady, catchy, high-pitched riff from a Farfisa organ drove the song along. She laughed when the track finished. 'That's great,' she said. 'What do you think?'

'Great,' I agreed.

'Could be our new single,' she said.

'It'll be a hit.'

'I hope so. I used to know him.'

'Who?'

'Bolan.'

'Did you?'

'Yeah. He had a hit in the States with *Bang a Gong* and a whole bunch of us formed a glam-rock band in LA. The lead guitarist and I came over and found Marc. He was a funny little guy. Pretty as hell but *really* weird, but in a nice way, y'know?'

I nodded.

'He took us out to dinner one night. It was a disaster. He always wore these little-girl shoes. He got them from Anello's. They were leather, with little heels and fastened with buttons. He told us that the English mod girls used to wear them in the sixties. He had about a hundred pairs, all colours. Trouble was, they had leather soles and heels. They were real slippy. We went to a restaurant on the King's Road. It was downstairs and Marc had had a bit to drink. The stairs were made of marble and he was walking behind me when he slipped and knocked me down, and I ended up on my ass in front of a whole restaurant full of people. I wasn't wearing *any* underwear. Boy, was I red! He was so mad he ran off and took the car, and I ended up in the middle of the street in the rain looking for a cab and crying my eyes out.'

'What happened?' I asked.

'I met a guy. We were together for three months. He picked me up in his car. Apparently Bolan, who's halfway home by this time, remembers me and gets his car turned around. He spent half the night driving round Chelsea looking for me.'

'And?'

'And I'm in bed with the guy I met.'

'What happened to the lead guitarist?'

'Met a guy too.'

'The lead guitarist was a woman?'

'No,' she said, and grinned. 'Anyway, Bolan delivered a ton of flowers to our hotel the next morning. I phoned him up and he said, "I'll phone you right back, I'm writing my next hit. I'll write one for you in a minute".'

'Did he?'

'Sure. We cracked the hundred with it about six months later. We were friends for years. I cried for a week when he died. He was coming over to visit. So doing that song on the album is just my way of letting him know I still care.' She pulled a mournful face, then looked through the window and her mood changed. 'Hey, we're here.'

And we were. The restaurant was in Greek Street. Chas stopped the car outside, hopped out and opened the door for us. Ninotchka led the way in. The greeter ran across the room like he was on elastic. 'Can we have a table?' asked Ninotchka. 'We haven't booked.'

'Of course, dear lady,' said the greeter who was a sixteen-stone Korean in a silk kimono. He started rapping out orders to the waiters who scuttled off to do as they were told. The greeter led us into the restaurant where the waiters were setting up a table next to an ornamental fountain. 'Best table in the place,' said the greeter. 'Private for conversation, but you can see who's in.' That had never been a priority in my book, but I nodded a thank you to him anyway.

We sat down like royalty and the waiters fussed around us. 'They'll choose, I haven't got a clue what to order,' said Ninotchka. She told the waiter to bring a selection of food and she chose the wine. I was feeling more and more like a spare part.

We started with martini cocktails, which were nothing more than vermouth sluiced over ice then drained off and neat gin added. They tasted like freezing rocket fuel and had about the same effect. The food arrived with the wine just as we finished the aperitifs. We started with dumpling soup with side orders of beansprouts, cabbage, spinach, pickled cabbage and Chinese leaves. Some of the vegetables were cool on the tongue, and some were so hot as to produce tears. Next we got a beef dish with broccoli and hard-boiled eggs. Then ox tongue and a dip of seasoned sesame oil. And finally squid in sweet and sour sauce. Jesus, it was good. We pigged out completely. I asked Ninotchka if she was worried about her figure. She asked me if I was worried about it. I said no.

We finished with fresh fruit and coffee liqueurs. By that time it was about ten, and I knew as much about Ninotchka as her agent. She was good company, witty in a bitchy way, with a fund of scandalous stories about the rich and famous. She name-dropped outrageously. If she'd had an affair with the subject of a story she went as coy as hell. She often referred to herself in the third person, especially when talking about her singing or acting. She was as tough as an old boot, as shallow as a crispy pizza, as hard as a diamond, and as sexy as hell.

I liked her, but I reckoned Lomax had been dead right. She was a dangerous woman, but I was flattered at being with her and the glances we were getting from the other diners. Fame can be as addictive as any drug, and I was being fed a good taste. I loved it.

When we'd finished every scrap of food on the table, she asked: 'Do you fancy a club?'

'Sure.'

'Great, I know just the place. It's right round the corner.'

I asked for the bill, but the greeter told me the meal was on the house. Ninotchka shrugged as if she expected nothing less. I took a mint for later.

When we got outside, the street was rotten with photographers. The greeter had done a job. We pushed through the *paparazzi* and the small crowd of gawpers that had gathered. I looked for one particular photographer I knew, but he wasn't about. We slid into the car and shut the door on the flowers of light that bloomed from the flash guns. 'Great,' said Ninotchka. 'I can still draw a bunch of those jerks.'

'Is that how you judge yourself?'

'In this business it's the only way. Why, don't you approve?'

'Sure, if it makes you happy.'

'It doesn't make me happy,' she said with an edge of anger in her voice. 'It's just how you judge fame. And fame is the name of the game.'

'Yes, Ninotchka.'

She changed mood mercurially again. Chas was driving us slowly round Soho Square. She rolled down the divider, 'Candy's,' she said. Candy's was a club off Wardour Street. It was in the basement of a dirty old building down a narrow alley that smelt of piss. It was not the most salubrious niterie in central London.

The woman behind the desk in the foyer of the club weighed about twenty stone and had poured herself into a black leather mini-dress fastened at the sides with criss-crossed black laces threaded through eyelets in the fabric. She was wearing nothing underneath and flesh bulged cruelly between the cords. She jumped up as Ninotchka and I pushed through the outside door. 'Darling!' she screeched at the top of her voice. 'So glad to see you again.' When she saw me, she did a double take. 'Who is this gorgeous man you've found? He's divine.'

I had to laugh. 'Hello, May,' I said.

'You know each other?' asked Ninotchka.

'Nick knows everyone,' said May.

'Everyone sleazy and perverted,' I said.

'It's your life.'

'Our life, May,' I corrected her. Then to Ninotchka: 'How do you know the place?'

'Everyone knows Candy's,' said May.

'Only lowlifes,' I said.

May pulled herself up to her full six foot two in spiked heels and posed with her fists on her hips. 'So what does that make you?'

'You tell me, May.'

She came around from behind her desk and enveloped me in blubber, giving me a big wet kiss on my mouth. 'Get in there and enjoy yourself.' To Ninotchka: 'Have a wonderful night, and look after this man.'

'I will.'

'How do you know this place?' I asked again as we went into the club proper and found a booth.

'I'm kinky.'

'Do you wear this sort of stuff then?' I asked.

'Sometimes. Do you?'

'No. I did a favour for May years ago. She's repaid the debt half a dozen times over. She treats me like a brother.'

'Really?'

'*Really*,' I confirmed.

I looked around and a waitress appeared. She was wearing six-inch-heeled shoes, fishnet tights, a leather corset with holes cut out to expose her nipples, and a leather G-string. She wore dead white make-up, black lipstick, thick sooty mascara, and her nails were painted with black nail varnish. The sides of her head were shaved and she had a Mohican dyed blue that stood at least eighteen inches high. She bent down and placed two fluted glasses on the table, showing off a cleavage you could lose your car keys in. I averted my eyes and remembered how embarrassing it could be to order a lager at Candy's. A long streak in skin-tight black leather and a Cambridge rapist's mask popped out from behind the bar with a bottle of champagne, which he opened with a flourish, not spilling a drop. 'On the house,' he said through the zipper on the mask. By the label on the bottle it was the good stuff that May kept for her special friends. The waiter poured us out two glasses and left with a swish of his hips.

'Tell me how you helped May,' said Ninotchka when we were comfortable.

'May is weird, right?' I said over Holly Johnson exhorting us to Relax, don't worry. 'She enjoys running this place, but she wants to earn too. So she lets the straights in here to blimp the freaks and spend eighty quid on a bottle of bad champagne. The main action takes place in the back room, for real *aficionados* only.'

'I've been in there,' she said.

I might have known it. 'And VIP guests,' I added.

'Have you been in there?' she asked.

'Yes.'

'Did it get you off?'

'No.'

'Too rich for your blood?'

'Not really. It just isn't my scene. All that rubber and leather and stuff looks like fun, but the people who wear it are all too bloody serious. Sort of, "Look at me, ain't I the horny one?" Anyway what happened was, someone was taking photographs and using the membership lists to get addresses and put the black on. You'd be amazed how respectable some of the people who come here wearing this kit are, and how much they'd be willing to pay to keep their names out of the papers. It's crazy. If it was me, I'd stay home and dress up in the bedroom, and no worries. But they've got to put it about. It was one of the barmen who was at it. It took me all of forty minutes to suss him out. He was real stupid. Now May thinks I'm the top man.'

'Her hero.'

'That's me,' I said, sipping at my drink. 'So listen, tell me about this guy Trash.'

'What about him?'

'Who would want him dead?'

'Anyone with any sense.'

'You don't like him.'

'No.'

'May I ask why not?'

'I don't like the way he came into the band and wanted to be the star. I made this band what it is today. Before I joined it was just a bunch of English guys playing twelve-bar blues. No money, no work, no record deal. Just a name that turned up on oldies stations once in a while. Then I joined, and my songs and my arrangements and my choreography saved their butts. Then Donny and Billy Joe got killed in that car wreck, and in came Trash. Trash by name, trash by nature if you ask me.'

'I do.'

'There it is then. And I don't want to talk about him any more. I want to have a good time.'

'Girls just wanna have fun, huh?'

'You said it, Buster.'

We finished the first bottle of champagne, then another. Ninotchka asked the barman what Bourbon they sold. By midnight we were drinking Rebel Yell with Budweiser chasers, or Budweiser with Rebel Yell chasers. Take your pick. By one, we'd graduated to Tequila Slammers. Around two the place did start to relax, don't worry, and someone started popping amyl nitrite in one corner which didn't help. The waitress with the Mohican took a crumpled joint out from between her breasts and gave me a blowback and all was mellow. I remember how hard her nipples looked poking through the holes in the leather and that was the last thing I *do* remember.

6

I woke up with a long, cold, steel rod running through my right eye and pinning the back of my skull to the pillow. I tried to turn my head and pain ran down the rod and I saw bright flashes of light behind my eyelids. I put my hand gingerly up to my eye and felt around. Nothing. Thank God, I thought, and opened my eyes, and wished I hadn't, and shut them again, tight. I lay wherever I was for a few more minutes and tried again. It was a little better. I gently hitched myself up on my elbows and looked around the room. I suddenly remembered where I was and the previous night and shuddered.

I was alone, lying on top of the bed dressed in just a pair of boxer shorts and one sock. My new clothes were strewn across the room. I licked my lips and gasped at the exertion. I rolled off the bed and stood up and the room started to spin. I went down on my hands and knees and crawled across the carpet, into the bathroom and over to the shower, opened the door, pulled myself up by the shower handle and turned the water on. I let it run hot, then cold, then hot again. I leaned against the wall and slid slowly down until I was curled up on the tiled floor. I reached up and adjusted the water to blood temperature and slipped down again, and lay as the water pounded on to me and down the drain.

I don't know how long I lay there. When I felt as if my skin was going to be washed down the drain too, I reached up and turned off the water. The bathroom was full of steam. I walked across the room, leant on the hand basin, rubbed the condensation off the mirror and looked at myself. It wasn't a pretty sight. I'd seen better ten-day-old corpses. I thought about a shave and thought about coffee. Coffee won. I wrapped myself in one of the towelling robes thoughtfully supplied by the management, and went through the bedroom to the sitting room and the telephone directory. I looked up room service and had started to dial when there was a knock on the door. I swore once, dropped the phone and answered. There was a roly-poly fellow outside dressed in a white shirt, brown bow tie and matching trousers. In front of him was a wheeled trolley covered with dishes with silver lids, plates, cups and saucers, and a coffee pot.

'Breakfast, sir,' he said with a smile.

I inhaled. 'Coffee.'

'Of course. A special breakfast blend I have made up specially.'

'How did you know?' I asked.

'I always think that a gentleman should breakfast by noon.'

'Christ,' I said, 'is it that late?'

'11.30, sir.'

'Come in.'

He wheeled in the trolley and my stomach rebelled at the smell of food. He pushed the trolley over to the dining table, took a folded white cloth off the trolley, shook it out and flicked it over the table. He laid out a knife and fork, breakfast cup and saucer, sugar and cream. 'What does sir require this morning?' he asked.

'Sir requires brain surgery,' I said. 'But coffee will do.'

'At once. Black or white?'

'White,' I said.

He picked up an electric percolator off the trolley and poured out a cup and added cream. 'Sugar?' he asked. It was like being back at Mum's.

'Two.'

He did as I asked, and I went over and slumped on a dining chair.

'And would sir care for one of these?' He took a box of paracetamol out of his shirt pocket.

'Yes, please,' I said. My head was still throbbing.

He took two from the box and dropped them into my palm. My hand was shaking but he was too polite, or well trained, or both to mention it. I swallowed one pill with a mouthful of coffee, then the other. The coffee tasted just like coffee is supposed to taste at a time like that. 'Something to eat?' he asked.

'I don't think so,' I said.

'Maybe some scrambled egg? Just right for a queasy stomach, especially with a dash of Worcester sauce.' He took a covered pan from the bottom of the trolley and whipped off the lid with a flourish. 'Perfect,' he said. 'They should always be taken off the heat and allowed to finish cooking in the pan. That way they don't get heavy. There's nothing worse in my opinion than heavy scrambled eggs.'

I didn't argue.

'This way they stay fluffy,' he went on.

He spooned a little egg on to a plate. It certainly looked fluffy enough. He removed the lids from the rest of the dishes like a conjuror. 'Bacon – grilled lovely and crisp. Mushroom, tomato, sausage, kidney.' As he spoke he added a little of each to the plate and placed it in front of me. It looked good and I felt a little better. I forked some egg and tasted it. It was delicious. 'This is great.'

'I'll leave you now, sir,' he said. 'If you need me I'm in my kitchen at the end of the corridor. I'm on until two this afternoon. My name's Wilfred.'

I was getting stuck into the breakfast. It was the best I'd had for ages and I told him so.

'Before I go, sir, I brought you up a couple of papers. I thought you might be interested.'

'I don't think so,' I said.

'Oh, I do, sir. Everyone was talking about it this morning.'

'It?'

He opened the *Sun* to the pop page. You know, where you can learn which star has had liposuction, or is gay, or a drunk.

Slap in the middle was a photo of Ninotchka and me leaving the Korean restaurant. It wasn't a bad photo of either of us. I could have done with a little more light on my left side, but otherwise OK. I was identified as the mysterious new man in her life seen dining intimately, etc, etc. 'You're right, Wilfred,' I said. 'I am interested.'

He showed me a couple of the other tabloids which both had variations of the same picture. 'You make a handsome couple, sir, if I may say so. Is there any chance of a permanent liaison?'

'You going to sell the story to Rick Sky?' I asked.

'As if I would, sir. Here at Jones' we are noted for our discretion.' He seemed genuinely upset.

'I'm sorry, Wilfred,' I said, and meant it. The guy had just saved my life single-handedly after all. 'I didn't mean to be rude.'

'Of course not, sir,' he said, brightening up somewhat. 'You weren't to know.'

'No permanent liaison,' I said. 'And that's official. In fact, I think I lost the lady at some point last night. You haven't seen her anywhere, have you?'

He looked around as if she might have been stashed in the kitchen cupboard. 'No, sir, but apparently she and her driver helped you into the hotel about 4 a.m.'

'Is that a fact?' I said. That bit hadn't come back to me yet.

'I wouldn't worry, sir,' said Wilfred. 'Worse things happen at sea.'

'Unfortunately I was supposed to be on dry land at the time,' I said.

'Quite so, sir. I'll leave you now. As I said, if there's anything you need, just ring.'

'Thank you, Wilfred.' And he backed out discreetly, leaving the trolley and the coffee pot with it.

Five minutes later there was another knock. 'Come in,' I said. The door opened and Róger Lomax entered. He was wearing the same style and colour jacket as I'd been wearing the previous night. Now I knew what Ninotchka meant about shopping in hotels. 'Morning,' I said.

'Barely.'

'Is that a rebuke?'

'I thought we were going to see Trash this morning.'

'What's stopping us?'

'The state of you.'

'Yeah, I know, I'm a mess.'

'This is a mess,' he said, and threw the paper down in front of me. It was the *Daily Mail*.

'I don't read shit like that,' I said.

'Read it this morning as a favour to me.'

I shrugged and picked it up. It was opened to the diary page and there, six inches deep and two columns wide, was a picture of Ninotchka and me coming out of the Korean restaurant again. I felt as if I had seen the movie. 'And I wanted discretion,' he said.

'No, you didn't,' I said back, tapping the paper. 'You wanted this.'

'What?'

'Someone noisy, who stomps around and flushes out whoever is lurking in the wood pile. That's what you wanted. If you'd wanted discretion you'd have called in Pinkerton's.'

At least he had the good grace to look a little sheepish. 'And another thing,' he said, 'what was the big idea of leaving her security man here at the hotel? Why do you think we go to the trouble and expense of hiring these guys? So that they can sit here and watch TV and eat fillet steak at sixty bucks a throw?'

'She didn't want him around,' I said.

'I don't give a shit what *she* didn't want. It's what *I* want that matters. Christ, from what I heard she carried you back here. What good would you have been if someone had been after her last night?'

There was no answer to that, so I didn't try.

'Jesus Christ, Sharman,' he said.

'Are you giving me my cards?' I asked.

'No,' he said. 'I've only myself to blame. I should have known that anyone McBain recommended was bound to be a flake.'

'Thanks,' I said.

'How long will it take you to get dressed?'

'Should be there by Christmas,' I replied.

'I'll meet you in the lobby in twenty minutes. Remember who's paying your wages.'

'Yes, sir,' I said to his back as he left the room.

7

I showed up present and correct, dressed in more new clothes, shaved and combed, in the lobby exactly nineteen and a half minutes later. Lomax was sitting in one of the overstuffed armchairs reading the US edition of *GQ* with one elegantly trousered leg crossed over the other. I was equally as elegant in a greeny-grey Valentino suit, cream shirt, and a silk tie whose pattern mimicked the interior of the succulent house at Kew Gardens.

'Very smart,' said Lomax.

'Hospital visiting,' I said. 'Got to look crisp.'

We drove to the Cromwell Hospital in another limo. This one was white. I felt like a bride.

We travelled the short distance in silence. Whether Lomax was deferring to my hangover, or whether he was still miffed and letting me know it, I don't know. Myself, I had nothing much to say. I sat and wondered what had happened to Ninotchka. I hadn't had a chance to find out before meeting Lomax. The car pulled up at the main door of the hospital and we both piled out. The entrance hall was as different from the entrance hall of an NHS hospital as it was possible to be while still in the same business. It was nearly as luxurious as the lobby at Jones'.

I hated it. I'd seen the insides of enough hospitals, especially casualty departments, to feel distinctly uneasy at the hush and the clean carpets and the corporate air of the place.

We checked in with a nurse in a Dior uniform and went to a lift that whisked us straight to the top floor. More carpet, luxuriant plants in terracotta pots, and a private room so full of flowers that I half expected the wholesalers from Covent Garden to come and make a job offer.

In the bed by the window lay a tiny man with a bush of coal-black curls. He was watching TV tuned in to an Italian soft porn quiz show on a cable channel.

He looked away from the screen as we entered. 'Check this fox,' he said. 'She's a housewife. Whoever wins the viewer vote gets ten free minutes in the Italian version of Safeway. Shit, I wish she was my old lady.' An extremely horny-looking blonde was just stepping out of her skirt. She was wearing a bustier, stockings and suspenders. As she bent down to untangle the hem from her stiletto heel, one pink-tipped breast popped out of her top. The game-show host was going mental, and Italian game-show hosts have got going mental down to the finest of fine arts.

The audience was cheering and I felt like joining in. Lomax picked up the remote from the bedside cabinet and hit the off button. 'Shit, Roger!' said the occupant of the bed. 'I was watching that.' I almost added that I was too, but thought better of it.

'Trash, meet Nick Sharman,' said Lomax.

'Hi,' said the man in the bed.

'Nick, this is Danny Shapiro – Trash to his friends.'

'How do you do?' I said.

'How British,' said Shapiro. 'You guys kill me.'

'Someone nearly did,' I said.

That brought the jollity level in the room down to a manageable level.

'Yeah,' said Shapiro.

'Who?' I asked.

He shrugged in his silk jammies.

You're a big help, I thought. 'Is your doctor about?' I asked.

'Sure,' said Lomax. 'On constant call. The prices we're paying…' He was getting tedious.

'Let's call him then.'

Lomax shrugged and walked out of the room. 'No idea?' I asked Shapiro.

'None, honest to God, man. I know this isn't the friendliest of businesses in the world, but murder…' He shuddered at the thought, and for a moment he wasn't a big, tough rock 'n' roller, just a scared geezer looking for justification. 'A joke or an accident, it had to be.'

I lifted an eyebrow. I'm quite good at it. 'Some joke,' I said. 'Where exactly did you get the gear?'

'Like I told Dodge and the Doc, I don't know.' He looked sincere enough, but somehow it just didn't ring true.

'Come on,' I said. 'Do you usually stick any old thing up your nose?'

'No, man, I get good stuff.'

'Usually.'

He nodded.

'It's strange that no one else took it,' I said.

'You know how it is. I stash a little here, a little there. For lean times, you know.'

I knew.

'So you think it might just have been lying around?'

'Could be.'

'Or did someone give it to you that night?' I asked. 'Just you. And watched you take it.'

'Maybe. Christ, I can't remember! I was so out of it.'

Terrific, I thought. The geezer's rotted his brain with drugs, and I'm supposed to get some sense out of him. Unless, of course, he was lying.

'Try and remember, will you?'

'I'll try. But, man, my mind's a blank.'

A not unusual state of affairs, I surmised. But even so, I wasn't sure that I believed him.

We were interrupted when Lomax came back with a slight, blond man with clear-rimmed spectacles and a clean white coat.

'Doctor O'Connell, Nick Sharman,' he introduced us.

'Can we talk, Doctor?' I asked. 'In private.'

The doctor took me out into the hall. 'Before we start,' I said, 'I know the ethics, but this could be attempted murder.'

'Don't I know it. I told them they should inform the authorities. They refused adamantly.'

'What was it?' I asked.

'I'll show you.' He took me along the corridor and into a small office containing just a desk, two chairs and a filing cabinet. He took a set of keys from his trouser pocket and opened a drawer in the desk. He took a white paper wrapping from the drawer. 'Heroin,' he said. 'His wife found this in the wastepaper basket.'

'Was there enough left to analyse?'

'Yes. Street grade. Maybe a bit better than that. But full of impurities. Caffeine, baby laxative, glucose... not a connoisseur's choice. In the parlance of the junkie, it's been stepped on heavily. If some of these people knew what they were taking...'

'If it had been pure?' I asked.

'Fatal.'

I nodded. I knew about pure horse.

'Is he a user?'

'No.' O'Connell shook his head adamantly. 'We've talked. I believe him. If he had been, it wouldn't have affected him so much.'

'Exactly what did happen?'

'The usual. Nausea, vomiting. He wanted to sleep, but thank God his wife had the presence of mind to keep him awake. If he'd gone into a coma we might not be talking now.'

'Is he all right now?'

'As all right as we can make him.'

'So he can leave?' I said.

'One more night should do it.'

'Good.'

I turned to go. 'Take care of him, Mr Sharman,' said O'Connell. 'Next time he might not be so lucky.'

I nodded and left. At the door I turned and said, 'Don't lose that,' referring to the sample he was still holding. 'We might need it later for evidence.'

'Trust me,' he said. 'I'm a doctor.'

'I'll do that.' I raised one hand in salute and went back to the room where Shapiro and Lomax were waiting. The quiz game was on again. Two naked women were rubbing what looked suspiciously like strawberry Fromage Frais into each other's breasts. 'The doctor's cool,' I said. 'He's given you a clean bill of health. You're leaving tomorrow.'

'That's right. Time's awasting and we've got lots to do.'

'OK,' I said, and then to Lomax, 'You'd better make sure this man of yours is covered with security from the moment he leaves here.'

'Like fleas on a dog,' said Lomax.

Shapiro pulled a face.

8

Lomax and I left soon after and drove back to the hotel. In the car he said to me, 'What do you think?'

'Dunno,' I replied. 'But I think he knows damn well where the smack came from.'

'Why?'

'Just intuition. I'm used to people telling me lies. I can pick them out of the air.'

'So why's he not telling?'

'Now *that's* the tough part. Have you got that list?'

'What list?'

'The list of everyone who was actually in the hotel the other night, and everyone who was hanging round your man's suite.'

'No. But Trash's old lady'll know. She's back at the hotel now.'

'What's she like?'

He looked towards the roof lining of the limo silently. His look said more than words could.

'OK,' I said. 'I get the picture. What's her name?'

'Lindy.'

'Nice.'

'Lindy Hopp with two "p"s. Ex-groupie.'

'Ex?' I asked.

'Sure. She got lucky. Married a rock star. Got the whole enchilada.'

'Are they OK?'

'How do you mean?'

'Together,' I explained.

'Oh, sure. As far as I know. Groupies are like geishas. They're versed in the art of pleasing men. That's their job.'

When we got back to Jones', we went straight to a suite on the third floor, in the far corner from Ninotchka's. Of her there was still no sign. We knocked on the door of the Bloomsbury Suite at about 1.15. Yet another security bloke came to the door. This one's name was Sam. He was big and black. I was beginning to wonder if anyone called Maurice or Oswald ever got into the security game, or if they all changed their names. 'Mr Lomax,' said Sam.

'Is Lindy in?' asked Lomax.

'Sure. Come in.'

Together we went into the sitting room. It was the same size suite as Ninotchka's. One door to the corridor, four other doors where mine had only two. I was beginning to feel deprived. There was a long skinny woman with black hair cropped close to the skull sitting on one of the sofas watching TV. She was wearing a green lurex top cut high at the neck and a short black skirt. There were two cocktail glasses on the low table in front of her, empty except for the dregs of some creamy-coloured drink. She looked happy enough about it. 'Hi, Dodge,' she said. She had an American accent. A real one as far as I could tell from two words.

'Lindy.'

'Who's your friend?' She looked up at me through her false eyelashes.

'Nick Sharman. He's a private dick.'

At the word 'dick' she raised her eyebrows. She couldn't have been more obvious if she'd had 'horny' tattooed on her forehead. 'Hi, Nick.'

'Hi, Lindy.'

'What can I do for you guys?'

'Nick wants to ask you some questions.'

'Sure, I've got nothing else to do except put another coat of varnish on my nails.' And she moved languorously on the cushion of the sofa. The way she said it and the way she moved I suddenly realised I liked her. Few Americans, and as far as I could see even fewer people in the rock business, could appreciate irony. 'Sit down, do,' she said. 'Sam, get my guests some drinks.'

I was beginning to like her more and more. I sat on the sofa opposite and I could see quite clearly up her skirt and that she was wearing red pants. Very small red pants. She knew I could see, and I knew she knew, and it seemed to suit us both just fine.

'What'll you have, gents?' asked Sam. I wondered if the guys from Premiere Security had to go on a bartending course before they qualified for their jobs.

'Gin and tonic,' I said. Lomax looked daggers at me. I ignored him.

'Beer,' he said.

'Get me another Brandy Alexander, Sam honey, will you?' said Lindy.

He went over to the bar and started rattling bottles.

'We've just been to see your husband,' I said.

'Great,' she replied without any real show of enthusiasm.

'He'll be home tomorrow.'

'Great.' Ditto.

'You're not pleased?'

'Sure. It'll be good to have Trash back. Then he's in the studio for a month, or rehearsing, or on tour. Fine. I see lots of him.'

'You could be with him now.'

'Who the hell are you to tell me where I can or can't be?' she said angrily, and closed her legs and pulled her skirt down. Which did nothing to improve the view.

Sam brought over the drinks. He gave me a mournful look as he gave me mine. I tasted it. It was fine. 'Thanks,' I said to his retreating back. 'Who was here when your husband snorted the smack?' I asked Lindy.

She thought for a moment. 'Trash, me, Pandora and his two little friends, Chick and Seltza.'

I lifted my eyebrows again.

'Roadies,' she said. 'We were partying.'

'Anyone else?'

'Seltza's old lady. His *English* old lady. What's her name, Dodge?'

'Patty,' said Lomax.

'And Chick had a chick with him.' She smiled a ghost of a smile. 'And Trash's dealer came by.'

'Does he have a name?' I asked.

Lindy looked at Lomax who nodded. 'Sandy,' she said. 'But I'm sure he didn't...'

'Someone did,' I said to her. 'Anyone else?'

'Sweetheart.'

'Who?'

'Sweetheart. She's a PR person with On Line.'

I looked at Lomax. 'They're our PR company over here,' he explained.

'And Turdo dropped by,' said Lindy.

'Who?' I said.

'Turdo,' said Lomax. 'Another roadie.'

'Sounds delightful,' I said.

Lomax and Lindy didn't comment.

'Was that it?' I asked.

'I think so,' said Lindy.

'I'd like to talk to them,' I said to Lomax.

'Sure. Anytime you like.'

'And this guy Sandy – how do I get hold of him?'

'He'll be around,' said Lindy.

'Not if it was him,' I said. 'But I'm sure we can find him, if we look really hard. On that night, did you notice anything strange?' I asked her. 'You know, before he got sick.'

'No. I was blasted. I didn't know what the hell he was doing.'

'And he got ill around three?'

'Yeah. I was right next to him in bed when he started thrashing about, you know.'

I could guess.

'You saved his life,' I said.

'A regular little Candy Striper,' she said sarcastically.

'You still did it,' I said. 'He owes you one.'

'He'll pay,' she said. And on that note I left it.

'Thanks, Lindy,' I said. 'You've been a big help. I might need to talk to you again. Is that all right?'

She nodded. 'I visited him yesterday,' she said.

'Sure. Roger, let's go.' And I put my glass on the table with the rest of the empties.

We left the suite and went back to the lobby. Ninotchka was at the desk with Don in close attendance. He looked at me like I'd just called his mother a rude name. Ninotchka looked on top form in a short strappy dress and a beaten-up denim jacket. 'Nick,' she said, 'I thought we were going shopping.'

Lomax gave me an old-fashioned look. It pissed me off. 'What's stopping us?' I said, and offered her my arm. 'See you later, Roger.' And Ninotchka and I left.

9

Don followed us. Obviously I wasn't going to be trusted as Ninotchka's sole bodyguard again. Considering I still couldn't remember getting back to the hotel the previous night, or morning, or whatever, I wasn't that surprised.

At the kerb outside, Chas was leaning on the wing of his limousine. I was beginning to get used to travelling in style, door to door, and fleetingly wondered how I would feel if I was ever forced to queue for a bus again.

Chas sprang to attention when he saw us and opened the back door of the car. He smiled as he greeted us. 'Good afternoon, miss. Sir.' Then to me: 'Fully recovered, I hope, sir?'

'Just about.'

'Don't tease him, Chas,' said Ninotchka. 'He wasn't himself last night.'

I wondered who I was then, but said nothing and followed her into the long passenger compartment of the car.

Don got into the front passenger seat and Chas got behind the wheel. He lowered the glass partition that separated us. 'Where to, miss?' he asked.

'Knightsbridge, opposite Harrods. That little shop we saw the other day, remember?'

'Of course, miss,' he said, and the partition rolled up again and we set off.

It only took a few minutes to get to Knightsbridge and it's surprising how good London looks on an early summer's afternoon through the smoked glass of a Cadillac sitting next to a beautiful, famous woman with her arm linked through yours. I can highly recommend it.

The car drew up opposite Harrods and Don nearly broke a leg getting the back door open for us. I let Ninotchka get out first and the sight of the curve of her bottom as she bent forward didn't hurt either. I joined her on the pavement. We were outside the chrome and marble front of a shop with a sign above the door that read FRONZOLI. Inside the window was a single navy blue blazer elegantly draped over some white-painted scaffolding poles. Nothing else. No price tag. Nothing. 'Nice,' I said.

'Not bad,' said Ninotchka. 'Let's see what else they've got.'

All three of us went into the shop. Ninotchka and I in the lead, Don two paces behind scouring the landscape for someone to beat up.

The atmosphere inside was hushed and reverent, with just the breath of a string quartet whispering through hidden speakers to interrupt the calm. The decor was minimal with black walls and more scaffolding supporting two suits. That was it. Just two. One white and one black. And nothing as vulgar as a counter or a till. It was a bit like walking into a monochrome photograph. There was a soft black leather sofa against the far wall. Perched on one arm was a slim, olive-skinned girl in a black dress. Standing next to her was a beautiful boy, with beautiful hair, beautifully styled. He was dressed in a twin of the black suit on the scaffolding teamed with a white shirt. Next to him was a shorter, older, fatter man almost bald on top with a long ponytail hanging down his back. He was wearing a white suit identical to the one on display with a black shirt underneath. I had to own up – the clothes the two geezers were wearing looked good, and I knew we were talking grands at least. All three looked at us as we entered.

The bald man recognised Ninotchka and ran the length of the shop towards us. 'My dear lady,' he cried. 'So soon. It's good to have you here again.' He had a heavy Italian accent. Whether it was real or fake I couldn't tell. He clasped Ninotchka's right hand in both his fat, dimpled paws and held it for at least half a minute, gazing up into her eyes as if speechless from her presence. All I could think was that she should count her rings when he let go. 'Divine,' he said. 'Divine. Today you look eighteen.' He slapped one hand to his forehead. 'What am I saying? Sixteen.'

Ninotchka lapped it up. She smiled shyly and I swear she even fluttered her eyelashes. Have you ever tried to do that? After all the bullshit was over, the greaseball copped a look at me out of the corner of his eye. I know that kind of look. The last time I caught one was from a geezer selling past their sell by date hamburgers off a van at Catford Dogs. He knew I knew it too. I think he might have winked. I've always thought it must be crap to be rich and have people con you lousy.

'To what do we owe the pleasure this bello afternoon, signorina?' he asked. "This bello afternoon." Was this guy real or what?

'Something for Mr Sharman,' said Ninotchka. 'Nick, this is Carlo.'

'Carlo Carruscore,' he said, and gripped my hand and shook it hard.

'Delighted,' I said.

'What exactly do you require?' He didn't ask me. He had the financial pecking order worked out to a T.

'Every style. Every colour,' said Ninotchka.

I looked at her. 'Hold on,' I said.

'Think Columbia,' she said back.

Carlo didn't miss a beat, just ushered me further into the shop and snapped his fingers at the beautiful boy. 'Geraldo!' he shouted. 'Measure.'

The beautiful boy produced a tape measure as if by magic and Carlo snatched it from him and snapped it around me, shouting measurements and comments in Italian as he went. Geraldo took notes on a pad he had produced from another pocket. When Carlo had finished he flung the tape around Geraldo's shoulder, and the two men, followed by the olive-skinned girl, vanished through an almost invisible door in the wall. I turned to Ninotchka.

'Listen, this is going to cost a fortune. Everything went up twenty-five per cent the minute you walked through the door.'

'I'm used to that, Nick,' she said. 'I don't care.'

'But, Ninotchka, I can't take a load of stuff off you. Maybe a nice tie.'

'Who gives a shit?' she said.

'I do. I'm not used to getting presents from women.'

'It's nothing.'

'It's going to cost a packet.'

'Peanuts, Nick. Trust me, I'm enjoying myself.'

I frowned and consoled myself that the clothes probably wouldn't fit. Carlo and Geraldo and the girl came back loaded down with gear. Although there were only three items on show, it seemed that the stock room was bulging. Carlo waved me through another almost invisible door into a mirror-lined changing room about the size of my hotel suite. There was no chance of barking your elbow at Carlo's place. The trio followed me carrying suits, jackets, shirts, leathers. Everything a boy could want. Ninotchka came too and I half expected Don to join us and give me some style pointers. The four of them stood and looked at me and I looked right back.

'Nick,' said Ninotchka.

'Ninotchka,' I said.

'Try something on.'

'With all you lot here?'

Carlo clapped his hands and saved the day. 'Outside, everyone. Give the signor some privacy.' They all left and I shut the door and picked up a shirt. The label read 100% silk. I slipped out of my clothes and put it on. It was beautiful. Then I tried on a wine-red single-breasted silk suit with a high-buttoning jacket. Every stitch was a work of art. I've never ever felt so good. It fitted like it had been made for me. I went outside to where the whole gang was waiting with bated breath. Carlo just about had an orgasm. 'Bella, bella, bella,' he cried as he raced around the shop almost beside himself with glee. 'Perfetto. Style, colour, cut. Perfetto.'

'You look good, Nick,' said Ninotchka.

'Like the president of Columbia Records?'

'Better. He's fat and bald with bad breath. Carlo, we'll take the lot.'

'No, we won't,' I said.

'*Nick!*'

'No. I can't take all this off you.' I touched the pop art tie I had on. 'I wouldn't say no to this though.'

'Nick, please.'

'No, Ninotchka.'

'But I thought…'

I pulled her away from the spectators. 'I only came with you to piss Lomax off. I can't take all this off you. It's too much, and that's final.'

'Peanuts,' she said again.

I shrugged.

She turned to Carlo. 'Wrap up the tie,' she said.

He did as he was told, but kept looking daggers at me from underneath his eyebrows.

I went back and got changed into my own clothes. When I returned to the shop no one was speaking. What could I do? Ninotchka tried to blank me as we left. 'Hey,' I said, 'I love the tie. I mean it. And you *do* have good taste in men's clothes. But maybe just a little rich for my blood.'

She smiled. She was a sucker for compliments.

'And now,' I said, 'I'm going to buy *you* a present.'

She stopped dead. 'What?'

'You heard.'

'No one buys me presents,' she said wistfully, like a little girl who'd missed her birthday.

'I do,' I said. 'Come on.' And I pulled her through a gap in the traffic and across to Harrods. Don nearly had a spasm as he was prevented from following by a cab turning left into Knightsbridge. Ninotchka and I dived through the front doors and I stopped her just inside. 'We'd better wait for him,' I said. 'He'll get the hump otherwise.'

'I love "Hump",' she said.

A moment later Don came charging through the doors, then skidded to a halt when he saw us waiting. 'Come on, Don,' said Ninotchka. 'You're getting slow.'

That comment didn't improve his temper or our relationship. But what the hell? You can't get on with everyone.

'So what's it going to be?' I asked. 'The place is yours.'

'Perfume,' she said. 'I just adore perfume.'

So we went to the perfume department. Ninotchka ran around from counter to counter like a kid. I watched her like a father. Don watched me life a wolf eyeing up a tasty morsel.

Of course they didn't have what she wanted. They wouldn't, would they? So we all had to troop round to the Chanel shop in Sloane Street, where they had *exactly* what she wanted. A bottle of Chanel Number 22. Quite a big bottle. I paid by credit card and tried to ignore the three figure total. Most expensive tie I've ever had.

When she had her parcel we went back to the car. Once we got inside she told me that we had to make a detour to the studio where the band had been recording, to pick up a tape of the final mixes and running order for one side of the album. On the way, she snuggled up close to say thanks for the present, and kissed me on the cheek. The kiss burnt my skin.

The studio was in Gunter Grove, an imposing three-storey Georgian detached house behind high walls, with broken glass set in concrete on the top of them.

Chas parked the Caddy on a side street, and Ninotchka and I, with Don a few steps behind us, went through the iron gates, up three stone steps and were buzzed into reception.

The receptionist greeted us like long-lost family, and called through to the studio on one of those phones designed to prevent anyone in the same room hearing what the caller is saying. Half a minute later a kid with a pudding-basin haircut, baggy trousers and a hooded top came through a set of heavy double doors, gave Ninotchka a look of pure hero worship and led us through to the inner sanctum.

We went down a long corridor and into a control room crammed with so much state-of-the-art equipment that I half expected to meet Kirk and Spock fresh from being beamed up from an alien planet.

Sitting in a comfortable-looking swivel chair in front of a control desk was a young blond guy in designer denims and cowboy boots. He was listening to a playback through speakers the size of cabin trunks at a volume that could have brought down the walls of Jericho, pushing faders and twiddling knobs like his life depended on it. As soon as he saw us, he hit a button and the sound died suddenly.

'Ninotchka,' he said. 'Good to see you. I've missed you.'

'I've missed you too, Tony,' she said. 'Nick, this is Tony Tune. He's the producer of our new album. Tony, this is Nick Sharman, a friend of mine. And you remember Don, don't you?'

'Sure I do. Hi, Don.' Tony Tune stood up and stuck out his hand towards me. 'Nick. Nice to meet you. Any friend of Ninotchka's…'

'Howd'y'do?' I said, and shook the proffered mitten.

'You're here for your tape,' he said to Ninotchka.

'That's right.'

He moved over to a shelf full of cassettes, ran his finger along and flipped one out. 'Here you go,' he said. 'All done and dealt with. Side two of the new album, in all its glory.'

'Thanks, Tony. You're a sweetheart.'

'For you, anything.'

'What was that you were listening to?' asked Ninotchka, gesturing at the huge speakers.

'An album I'm doing for Epic. Some band they've dug up. Not in your league. You've got no worries there.'

'Well, we'll leave you to it,' said Ninotchka. 'Thanks for this.' She held up the tape. 'And I hope we'll be back to work soon.'

'How is Trash?' asked Tony.

'Much better, I believe.'

'Great. You know I'm yours at a moment's notice,' he said, and went back to his chair.

'Bye now,' said Ninotchka.

Tony winked, and before we were out of the door had put the music back on and was lost in the intricacies of the mixing desk again.

The three of us went back to the car and Chas drove us to the hotel. When we arrived I asked Ninotchka to join me for a drink. She said she didn't want to go to the bar so we went to my room. She told Don to wait in her suite. He started to argue, but thought better of it and left.

'At last,' said Ninotchka. 'I thought we were never going to get a chance to be alone.'

I can't tell you how flattering hearing something like that from a woman like that can be. I knew I was doing exactly what Lomax said I would do, and I didn't give a damn. At least I'd refused the clothes.

Ninotchka took off her jacket and threw it across a chair, and sat on the sofa showing plenty of leg as she did. I asked her what she wanted to drink. 'Can you do a Bloody Mary?' she said.

'The best in London.' I went to the bar, took a large jug and poured in two measures of sherry, eight of vodka, added a handful of silver-skin onions, lemon juice, splashed in some Tabasco, lots of Worcestershire sauce, a shake of celery salt, a sprinkle of pepper, loads of ice, and topped it up nearly to the brim with Clamato juice from the fridge. I stirred the whole lot thoroughly and poured two tumblers full through a big strainer. I tasted mine. Perfect. I added some more ice cubes to each glass and took them over to where she was sitting. 'Try that, and weep,' I said.

She took a sip and pulled a sour face. 'Perfect.'

'Not too much spice?'

She shook her head. 'If it don't bite, it ain't right.'

'Couldn't have put it better myself.'

'You have hidden talents.'

'Only when it comes to mixing drinks.'

'I'm sure that's not true. And that's something I want to talk to you about.'

'Really?'

'Really,' she said, and patted the cushion on the sofa next to her. 'Sit down.'

I did as I was told.

'Got any cigarettes?'

I produced a packet of Silk Cut.

'I said cigarettes,' she said. 'Haven't you got any American?'

'No. Do you want me to phone down?' I was getting used to this room service lark too.

'No, don't bother. I'll have one of those. But I don't know how you guys can taste them.'

I felt like apologising for Messrs Benson & Hedges but lit her a cigarette instead. She pulled a face as she inhaled but smoked it anyway. I lit one for myself and pulled an ashtray close to the edge of the coffee table. 'So what do you want to talk about?' I asked.

'You,' said Ninotchka, and fixed me with an appealing look that I was beginning to recognise. 'Do you enjoy what you do?'

I looked at her. I didn't, as a matter of fact, but I wasn't going to tell her. 'It's what I do.'

'Would you be interested in doing it specifically for me?'

'That's what I seem to be doing right now.'

'No, I mean *exclusively.* Come and work for me, Nick.'

'Doing what?'

'Whatever I want.' She sat back and sipped her drink.

'You're the second person to ask me that in a year,' I said.

'Who was the other?'

'A girl I used to know. She was a model. She wanted to be a singer. Funny that.'

'She must have seen the same things in you as I do.'

I shook my head. 'No,' I said. 'She thought what I do is too dangerous.'

'Is it?'

'It has its moments.'

'And?'

'And what?'

'What did you say to her?'

'I'm here now, aren't I?' I said. 'I told her no. That's why she's someone I *used* to know.'

'What's she doing now?'

I shrugged. 'I don't know.'

'Is there anyone else?'

'No,' I said. 'I cleared the decks. I'm all alone now.'

'Are you happy about that?'

I shrugged again. 'You get used to it.'

'I don't. I hate it.'

I thought about all the newspaper stories I'd read about her and men. 'I'm sure you don't have to be.'

As if she knew what I was thinking, she said, 'I'm terribly lonely, Nick. I'm always reading about how I'm screwing some guy or other. Most of them I've never met, or just said hello to at some party or other. Jesus, if I'd had as many fucks as the papers say, my pussy would be worn down to the bone.' She laughed and stubbed out her cigarette.

I had to laugh too. I wouldn't have minded the job as it goes, but I knew I couldn't accept. I liked her too much for one thing, even though I was beginning to realise what a manipulative bitch she was. And for another I could still feel the kiss she'd given me in the back of the car.

'So whaddya say, Nick?'

'I've got a job,' I said. 'Here, with you lot. I've already been paid. And I'm not doing it very well. Why would you want me to work for you?'

'I like you.'

'I like you too,' I said. 'Why don't we just keep it like that? I'm a bad employee on a permanent basis. I don't relate well to authority. It's better if I just freelance. Less stress on everyone.'

'It wouldn't be like that.'

'That's what all prospective bosses say.'

'I mean it.'

'Listen, Ninotchka,' I said, 'I think you're great. But that doesn't mean I want to belong to you. I'll be close until we find out what's happening here. I feel bad about taking money from the band and doing nothing in return.'

'What we paid you is chump change,' she said spitefully. Rich people *always* do that.

'See what I mean?' I said. 'As soon as we start talking money, everything changes.'

'I'm sorry, Nick,' she said. 'I'm just being an asshole. I'm used to people doing what I want.'

'I'm sure you are. But don't let's fall out.'

'Dinner tonight?'

'You're persistent.'

'I'm trying.'

'There's a million guys…'

'Sure,' she interrupted. 'But you're the one I want to have dinner with.'

'Let me see Lomax first. I'd better make my peace.'

'Call me in my suite?'

'Course I will.'

'Promise?'

'Promise.'

'Walk me down.'

'It'll be a pleasure.'

We got up and somehow she was in my arms and we were kissing. Jesus, it was like having a butterfly in my mouth. Then she pulled away. 'Sorry,' she said. 'I shouldn't have done that. I'll see myself to my room.' And she ran out and slammed the door behind her.

10

I found Lomax in the bar. Once again he was alone in the dark with an exotic cocktail in front of him. 'Still with us, Sharman?' he asked.

'I want to talk to you about that.'

'Talk away.'

'I've done a rotten job,' I admitted. 'No job in fact.' I stood there in silence for a minute, feeling like a fool. 'There's two reasons for that,' I said. 'One is that I don't like what I do anymore. Snooping around. Ferreting. And then opening a can of worms that won't be closed until someone else gets hurt.'

'Or you.'

'Or me,' I agreed. Then I was silent again.

'And the second reason?'

'You get right up my nose, as it happens.'

I couldn't see the expression on his face in the dimness of the bar, and I could not have cared less what it was. He reached over and turned up the light and looked at me. Then he laughed.

'You're honest, I'll say that for you.'

'I try to be.'

'So you want to quit?'

'No. There's a couple of people I've met here I like, and I took on the job, and I took your cash and clothes. Now I'll do what I came to do if you still want me around. Otherwise a full refund can be arranged.'

'No need,' he said. 'Stick around.'

'Thanks. I'm sorry I've wasted a day.'

'Forget it. All's quiet.'

'At the moment.'

'Security's tight.'

'You can say that again.'

'Premiere's a good company.'

'Yeah. The size of some of those guys! I don't know what they do to anyone with any funny ideas, but they sure scare the hell out of me.'

He laughed again. 'Between you and me, me too. And I pay their wages.'

'I was out of line leaving Don behind last night.'

'No problem. Like I said, all's quiet. So what are you going to do first?'

'The same as I said before. Talk to people.'

'Stick around then. The afternoon shift should be in soon. I'm surprised they're not in here by now.'

As if to confirm this, the door to the bar opened and three big geezers came in. They were strangers to me.

'More roadies,' said Lomax.

'I recognise the type.'

'Start with them,' he said. 'But watch them. They can be a bit...' he hesitated, '... abrasive around strangers. Yes, abrasive is the word. They were the ones that were in Trash's suite that night.'

'Is that so? Interesting. Yes, I'd like to talk to them.'

'Fine, but just remember they can be very difficult if you rub them up the wrong way.'

'I'll take the risk,' I said.

Lomax stood up and gestured the roadies over and they collected a beer each from the bar and came and joined us. They looked at me like I was an insect in the toilet bowl. 'Nick Sharman,' Lomax introduced me.

One of the roadies, a bear of a man wearing a baseball cap with the peak over one ear, said: 'We heard. Chippy told us.' He was American.

'Seltza,' said Lomax. 'Guitar roadie.'

I nodded at him.

'Turdo, drums,' said Lomax, and indicated the man on Seltza's right. He was very big too, with long, greasy hair tied back behind his ears. He didn't even bother to nod.

'Chick,' said Lomax and nodded at the last of the trio. This one was very tall with an acne-scarred face, denim shirt and jeans and thick red braces. His eyes flicked over at me and he drank some beer. Friendly guys, I thought.

'Chick's the best rigger in the business,' said Lomax by way of explanation. I wondered what a rigger was, but didn't ask. 'Nick wants to ask you some questions,' Lomax continued. 'Tell him what he wants to know. He's on our side.'

I got the impression that the three other men at our table thought differently.

'Well, guys, I've got to love you and leave you,' said Lomax. 'Things to do, people to see.' He stood and Turdo moved to let him out. 'Have fun,' he said to me.

I guessed this was his way of getting his revenge. After he'd gone there was silence. I looked at the members of the road crew. I said to Seltza, 'You were up in Shapiro's suite on the night he got poisoned?'

He shrugged. 'Sure.'

'Did you notice anything?'

'Like what?'

'Anything strange.'

'I was wasted, man. I didn't notice anything.'

'Except Lindy's tits,' said the one they called Turdo. He was American too, with an accent that sounded like it had crawled out of the Everglades on the back of an alligator. Eventually I was going to have to ask him about that name.

Seltza flashed him an angry look.

'Been on the road long?' I asked.

'Yeah, man,' said Turdo. 'Fucking forever.'

'Good band to work for?'

'They'll do 'til something better comes along.'

'Did *you* see anything the other night?'

'I wasn't around for long,' said Turdo. 'I had to visit a friend.'

'An errand of mercy,' said Seltza.

'She was sick,' said Turdo.

'And you rushed to her bedside,' said Seltza. 'And ended up in it.'

'She'd have to be sick to go to bed with that,' said Chick, speaking for the first time. He had a Scottish accent. All three laughed and slapped palms. Very macho. I was starting to lose interest, and I was the only one without a drink.

I looked at Chick. 'You were there too, weren't you?'

'Surely was.'

'See anything?'

'The same as him.' He indicated Seltza.

'So none of you saw anything?' I persevered.

'Looks like it.' Seltza again.

'Thanks,' I said. 'You've been a big help.'

'Sarcastic guy,' said Chick.

I tried a different tack. 'Did any of you know a bloke called Alan Gee? Algie. He was a road manager.'

Turdo snickered. 'Road manager.' He mimicked my London accent. That went down well, I can tell you.

'Mark McBain's personal?' said Chick.

I nodded.

'Who the fuck are we talking about?' asked Turdo.

'You remember him,' said Chick again. 'Big mother-fucker. Used to work for *Queen*. He came to that fucking open-air gig we did in Houston. Where it rained.'

'First day it rained in a fucking year,' said Turdo reminiscently. 'And it had to be on us. I remember. What happened to him?'

'He was killed by some nutty fucking Yank. Fucking Americans! Algie was a good guy. Outstanding,' said Chick.

'I was with him,' I said.

'When?' asked Chick.

'When he died. He saved my life.'

'That was you? Man, I read about that shit. It was all to do with

McBain, yeah? I met him once. Crazy fucker, man. Always high. Christ, man, that was a shame.'

'It was,' I said. 'Algie was a friend.'

'So?' asked Turdo.

Chick put up his hand to quieten him. 'Algie was cool. Didn't take no bullshit. Why'd he do it? Why'd he die for you?'

I shrugged. 'No idea,' I said. 'I never got to know him as well as I would have liked. But you're right, he didn't take any bullshit. It wasn't the only time he helped me. Someone close died and he was there for me.'

'A fucking lot of people round you die,' said Seltza.

I didn't answer that.

'So what are you getting at?' asked Chick.

'Nothing really,' I said. 'I know you don't want me round here. Nor did Algie when I went and worked for McBain. But I am here. I'm a fact of life. Like piles. He got used to me. We ended up friends. He had a good attitude. I wondered if you lot knew him and were the same, or if you were just going to wank around and hope I took umbrage and left. Because I won't, I promise you that. Also I wanted you to know that I'm not here to interfere in your lives – unless you gave Shapiro the heroin that nearly killed him. Maybe we can sort this all out with minimum trauma. But if something else bad happens the police will be called in and they tend to frown on certain recreational habits.'

'Like?' asked Seltza.

'Drugs.'

'The man's suggesting we take drugs,' said Chick. But his tone was noticeably lighter than previously.

'I think we should see a lawyer, man,' said Turdo. 'That's defamation of character.'

'You ain't got no character to defame, man,' said Seltza and finished his beer. 'Anyone for another?' he asked.

Both the other roadies lifted their glasses in assent. 'Wanna beer?' he said to me.

'Sure,' I said, and the ice was broken.

11

I spent the rest of the evening with the roadies. We ate dinner in the hotel restaurant. Keith Pandora was in with his two playmates, and another woman who resembled an older, ravaged version of them whom I took to be their mother. She was a flower child gone to seed, with straight hair too black to be natural and too long for her age. She wore a vaguely bohemian outfit of dark patterned long-sleeved shirt, worn loose over a mini skirt and black tights, with high-heeled boots, lots of silver, and a crystal on a chain around her neck. I disliked her on sight.

On their way out, Pandora stopped over at our table and spoke to me. 'I've been expecting a visit,' he said.

'You're next on my list.'

'When?'

'Tomorrow?'

'Sure. Come up at eleven and have breakfast.'

'OK. I look forward to it,' I replied. I could see the woman clocking me through the short conversation. The two teeny boppers looked bored throughout, and drifted away towards the exit.

'Aren't you going to introduce us, Keith?' asked the woman.

'Sorry,' he said. 'Nick, this is Andrea Batiste. Andrea, Nick Sharman.'

'Nice to meet you,' I said. Although it wasn't particularly.

'And you,' she said, and smiled. She looked younger when she did.

'Tomorrow then,' said Pandora, and they moved away. As they went Andrea Batiste looked over her shoulder at me.

When they were safely through the door, Seltza said, 'Shit! I couldn't tell you what I could do to those two little honey bunnies.'

'Man,' said Turdo, 'I'd love to have the pair of them in the shower, soaping me up and jerking me off.'

'Soapy tit wank,' said Chick, with a faraway look in his eyes.

'You fuckers are disgusting,' I said.

'Hey, Mr Straight, loosen up,' said Seltza. 'They love it as much as that hairy fucker Pandora. Come on, man. Don't tell me it hasn't crossed your mind. That you haven't thought about it a bit. Everyone else round here has.'

To be honest I had, and that's what I didn't like. I'll admit that the thought of those two lithe young bodies all over me like a rash turned me on. Then I thought about Judith and I felt ashamed. 'Sure,' I said, 'I've thought about it. And then after I've thought about it, I've thought how it would be if it was *my* little girl in a couple of years. Know what I mean?'

The table fell silent. 'Sure,' said Seltza after a moment, raising his hands in surrender. 'Nothing personal, partner.' He pronounced it, 'podner'. 'Didn't mean to give you a hard time. Subject closed. I didn't know you had a kid of your own.'

'How could you?' I said. 'Forget it.'

So he did and we ordered another round of drinks.

'So what about this band then?' I said. 'What's the full SP?'

'Come again,' said Seltza.

'Starting price,' I explained. 'A horse-racing term. I mean, what's the story from the beginning?'

'Shit,' said Seltza. 'How long you got?'

'Long enough. Tell me.'

'I'll tell you one thing,' said Chick, 'this is the dyingest band in the world. Trash was real lucky.'

'No, man,' said Turdo. 'This ain't the dyingest band. The unluckiest, yeah, but the dyingest, no.'

'Who then?' said Chick.

'*T-Rex*,' said Turdo. 'All them mothers dead.'

'*Lynyrd Skynyrd*,' said Seltza. 'Or *The Allman Brothers*.'

'How about *The Bar-Kays*?' said Turdo.

Chick thought about it. 'OK, maybe they ain't the dyingest band. But they're fucking close.'

'Tell me about it,' I said.

'Christ!' said Chick, and started ticking off on his fingers. 'The first drummer they had took too much acid and freaked out. One guitarist joined The Moonies. Another ended up in a mental hospital.'

'No, man, that was another drummer,' interrupted Seltza. 'That crazy fucker Bobby Boyle, or whatever the hell his name was.'

'Two drummers ended up on the funny farm,' said Chick. 'But they let Boyle out again. I was talking to Roger the Dodger about it.'

'Carry on,' I said.

'Two of them died in a car crash. They were racing Corvettes to Las Vegas for the pink slips. Neither of the fuckers would give way. One keyboard player OD'd after a week. He couldn't stand the pressure. He was only eighteen. Never been away from home. Seven days on the road with *The Box*, and the cat's dropping 'ludes like there's no tomorrow. One morning he just never woke up. Then Jackie Mulligan, played bass, took angel dust with Pandora. They found the poor fucker face down in the parking lot. He was so crazy he'd stuck his head under the wheels of a Mack truck.'

'Strictly speaking that wasn't an OD,' said Seltza. 'The verdict was suicide.'

'Same thing,' said Chick wisely. 'Sapperstein crashed his plane, and Griff Fender got electrocuted on stage. This band's had more members than the fuckin' Boston Philharmonic.'

'How many?' I asked.

'God knows. Seventeen... eighteen.'

'Maybe you're right, Chick,' said Turdo. 'Maybe this is the dyingest band.'

We all cogitated on that remark for a while.

'So listen,' said Seltza, changing the subject, 'who's coming up to get shit-faced in my little corner of the world? I've got some outstanding grass.'

Turdo said he was going to call up his girl and see what she was doing, Chick said he'd be delighted, and I tagged along for the ride.

Seltza's room was just that – a room. But a decent double and pretty luxurious. He'd installed a stereo compact disc player and stuck on the first *Doors* album.

He adjusted the volume and pulled a tray with papers and a bag of grass in it out of one of the drawers of his bureau.

'Trouble with CDs is there ain't room to roll a joint on the cover,' he said. 'Give me a regular album anyday.'

'It's the march of technology, man,' said Chick.

I was beginning to realise that Chick was something of a philosopher in his own, individual way.

Seltza made the joints American-style. All grass. One skin. No cardboard filter. Just a flat fold at the end. He rolled one, lit it, took a hit, passed it to Chick and started rolling another. 'Help yourself to a drink, Nick,' he said. 'The ice-box is full.'

I went over to the mini-bar and got a Grolsch. Chick asked for one too. Seltza went for a Bourbon on the rocks. I got the drinks and swapped them for the joint. I took a hit, and kept the smoke down for a long time before releasing it. The taste reminded me of other times. So did the music. I took the bottle and the spliff and sat on an easy chair by the window. The evening was warm, and the sky was growing dark and merging with the tops of the trees in the square across from the hotel. Between tracks on the album I could hear traffic and the sound of children going home. I drifted away as the dope took hold. My thoughts were like a kaleidoscope, jumping from one memory to another. So many people. So many gone. And not enough time or energy left to start again.

'Don't bogart that joint, my man,' said Seltza.

I came back to reality with a start. 'Sorry,' I said, took another hit and passed the joint to him. I looked at my watch. It was almost nine o'clock. Seltza went back to the bureau and brought out a bag of white powder big enough to choke a horse, and started cutting out long fat lines on the glass top. He took out a twenty and rolled it up into a tight tube. 'Guys,' he said, 'be my guests. Shorty laid this shit on me today. Best pink Peruvian.'

'Are you sure?' I said. My voice sounded stoned and I had some trouble enunciating the words.

'Yeah, man,' said Seltza. 'I gave it the test. It's good pure shit. Take my word.' As if to show his faith in the product he scarfed up the first line. 'Fuck!' he said after a moment. 'Awesome. Do your nose some good.'

He passed the rolled-up bank note to me and I took up a line myself. It made me go cross-eyed, and I felt that old familiar shiver go down my spine. 'Good gear,' I said, and Chick passed me a joint and dived into the Charlie. I drank more beer, sucked a mouthful of smoke and sat down again.

'What the fuck are we going to do?' asked Chick as he rubbed his nose.

'Want to boogie?' said Seltza.

'Who's on?' Chick again.

'*Cheap and Nasty*'s at the Astoria. *Fields of Nephelim* at the Town & Country. There's a party for *The Nasties* after.'

'The Astoria it is then,' said Chick. 'That way we can get out of it for nixes after. You know the tour manager, don't you, Seltz?'

'Sure,' said Seltza. 'The cheap bastard owes me. You coming, Nick?'

'No,' I said. 'I've got things to do tomorrow. It sounds like you're going to make a night of it.'

'Every fuckin' night,' said Seltza. 'Another time then?'

'Sure.'

'There's a reception on tomorrow for *The Miracle*. They've got a new album out. Want to come?'

'Where?'

'Inn On The Park, I think. I've got an invitation somewhere. Everyone's going, including your friend Ninotchka.'

'I'll be there,' I said.

'I bet you will,' said Chick. 'Be there or be square.' And he laughed a stoned laugh.

'Listen,' I said, 'I'll see you guys later. I'm going to wander about. See what's cooking.'

'Have fun,' said Seltza.

'That's what life's about,' said Chick. 'Don't do anything I wouldn't do.'

'Or anyone,' said Seltza.

'Yeah,' I said. 'G'night. And thanks for the dope.'

'Pleasure,' said Seltza. 'The pharmacist is always in attendance.' And he laughed too,

I left the room and went up to my suite. I went in, put on the TV, made a weak vodka with tonic and stretched out in front of the box.

I sat there for an hour or more, watching anything. Seeing nothing. Just coasting on a high, topping it up from the vodka bottle and drifting like a dead leaf on a current of warm air. Then the phone rang.

I picked up the receiver and it was Ninotchka. 'Where the hell are you?' she asked angrily.

'Right here. Where else?' I replied.

'I thought we had a date?'

'I got involved.'

'Fuck involved. Get up here now.'

'Hey, slow down,' I said. 'Not so fast. I've been working.' And I wondered why the hell I was justifying myself.

'Here. Now,' she said, and put the phone down in my ear.

His Master's Voice. Son, this is the record biz, I thought. I got up, put on my jacket and took myself and a mild cocaine hangover to face the music.

Don let me in to her suite. Ninotchka was sitting on the sofa. She was wearing a short black skirt and a dark green Levis shirt. Her legs were bare. 'Don, get lost,' she said.

'You know what Mr Lomax said,' he protested.

'Fuck Mr Lomax! Get the fuck out of here and stay out,' she hissed through clenched teeth. She looked and sounded strung out as hell.

'What about...'

'Just do it!' she shouted.

Don shook his head and left. 'I'll be right here,' he said as he closed the door behind him.

I lit a cigarette. Coke does that to me, makes me into a three packs a day man. Ninotchka sat and gave me the old snake eye.

'So where were you?' she said.

'With the road crew, getting fucked up,' I said, honesty being the best policy.

'Fine. You'd rather be with those creeps than me?'

'No. I was just getting acquainted. I have a job to do. Time flew. You know how it goes when you're having fun.' I was beginning to feel a bit strung out myself.

'Shit!' she said. 'Shit! Shit! Shit!'

I leant against the wall and smoked my cigarette.

'Get me a drink,' she said. No 'please', you'll notice.

'What?' I said. Meaning what drink, not that I hadn't heard her.

'Vodka and grapefruit. Have you eaten?'

'Sure,' I said. 'With the crew.'

'Christ, are you in love with those guys? You been jerking each other off, or what? I haven't eaten a fucking thing all day.'

'Call room service. Get them to kill the fatted calf,' I said.

'Why are you so horrible?' she said, and burst into tears.

Ah, tears. Don't you just love 'em?

I ignored her sobs and went to the bar. I made her a drink and took it over to her. 'Sorry, I haven't got a hankie,' I said.

'Get lost.'

'Just now you wanted me here. Now you want me to get lost. I wish you'd make up your mind.'

She looked up at me. Her eyes were dry and her make-up wasn't even smudged. 'I'm sorry, Nick,' she said. 'You're right. You've got a job to do. I'm just so uptight with all this waiting around.'

'Shapiro is coming out of hospital tomorrow. He'll be back at work soon.'

'Thank God for that. I'll go crazy if I have to stay here much longer with nothing to do.'

'Do you want me to order you some food?'

She shook her head.

'What then?'

'Stay with me. Keep me company.'

'Sure.'

So I stayed. But she was jittery and irritable. Not at all the same woman she'd been that afternoon, or the previous evening. Something was up, and I didn't know what. I still had a hangover from the joints and coke and booze I'd had earlier. She got up and started pacing the room. She switched on the stereo and sorted through the little silver discs looking for something. 'Fuck!' she said. 'Where is that fucking thing?'

'What?'

'That fucking *REM* album. I had it. I had it! I'm sure I had it.'

'Relax,' I said. 'It'll be there.'

'Some help you are,' she said. 'Find it for me.'

I went over. '*Document*?' I said.

'That's the one.'

'It's right here.'

'Put it on then.'

There was a knock at the door and Don stuck his head round.

'Can I see you?' he said.

She went to the door and stood blocking my view of what went on. When she turned round she looked happier. 'Put it on, Nick,' she said. 'I've got to go to the bathroom.'

'OK,' I said, and slipped the disc into the machine and pressed the play button. Michael Stipe started singing *Finest Worksong*, and I went and got a drink and lit another cigarette. The album played on and she didn't come back.

After about twenty minutes I went looking for her. I knocked on the bedroom door. No answer. It was locked. 'Ninotchka,' I called. Nothing. I rattled the door knob loudly. Nothing again. Shit, I thought.

I stepped back and hit the door with my shoulder. It was thick and heavy and bounced me back, and I knew that in the morning I was going to have a sore shoulder. I hit it again, harder, and heard something crack. Once more and the lock gave and the door crashed back against the wall.

I went into the room. There was one bedside lamp lit. The bed was made. Ninotchka was lying on it. Her skirt had been pulled up to her waist showing she was wearing lacy black bikini panties underneath. She was holding a loaded syringe in her right hand. The point of the needle caught the light from the lamp. 'You needn't have broken down the door,' she said. 'I was just going to come and let you in.'

'So that's why you were so fucked off?' I said. 'Waiting for the man.'

'And he came through,' she said lazily. 'Which is more than you have. D'you want a hit? Get you relaxed. In the mood.'

'No thanks,' I said. 'It's not my style.'

12

I watched as Ninotchka pumped up a vein in her thigh, and slid the needle on to the blue line under the skin, and I remembered the first time I ever saw anyone mainline. I only have to see a needle to remember. I was sixteen and still at school. It was the fag end of the sixties, and the hippies were getting dog-eared and ratty around the edges. I was hanging out with a weird bunch of ex-mods and soon-to-be glam rockers, with the odd skinhead and bike boy thrown in for flavour. They were mostly older than me, and I found them as glamorous then as I found them dull and stupid a couple of years later.

There was a girl. No, a woman, twenty-two or -three, who we used to run into down Streatham High Road. We'd meet her at the bowling alley or The Golden Egg. She wasn't with us, but we all knew her. I thought she was real sexy. She came from somewhere in the country and still had traces of the accent. But I never took the piss. To me then, not taking the piss was love. Still is, as it goes.

She was tall and built solid. Big shoulders, big hard breasts, and wide hips. But her legs were long and shapely. Not solid at all. She was blonde, but I guessed it was from the bottle and dreamed about finding out the one sure way. Her hair was chopped all ragged, like she did it herself, and she wore pink lipstick and thick, dark make-up to cover the acne scars on her face.

She worked in a garage in Brixton, on the pumps, and rode a motor bike.

She doesn't sound like much, but when I was sixteen she had the power to drive me crazy, and her deep, dirty laugh got me hard in a second.

One day that summer I was standing all alone in Norwood Road when she pulled up on her bike and asked me if I had any cash. I had, a couple quid change from posting some parcels for my father. I lent it to her. I would have cut my throat if she'd asked me to.

She told me to come down to the garage on Friday at four when she got paid, and she'd give me the money back.

I told my dad I'd spent the money, and got a bollocking, and promised to pay him back out of the wages from my Saturday job. I hopped the wag from school that Friday afternoon and went home and changed into some killer flared jeans and a tank top. Suave or what? I hooked a pair of John Lennon sunglasses over my ears and headed for the garage.

When I got there she was just finishing work and smelled of petrol and sweat and patchouli oil. She was wearing a pink Angora sweater, skintight jeans and bike boots. I hooked my thumbs over the waistband of my jeans and let my hands cover my erection.

'Hello, Nick,' she said. 'Come for your money?'

'Please,' I said.

She opened her pay packet and took out two pound notes and handed them over. 'Thanks,' I said.

'Thank *you*. You saved my life the other day.' She didn't elaborate, and it never would have occurred to me in those days to think how cheap her life must have been.

'Anytime,' I said, and blushed.

'What are you doing now?' she asked.

'Nothing.'

'Come back to my place for a cuppa?'

That was bliss. That was *it*. I had to sit down or I'd bust my jeans. 'Sure.'

'Maybe we'll get some beer later.'

She could bathe in beer if she wanted. Well, at least as much as two quid could buy.

She got her bike and I rode pillion. Rode pillion with my arms around her waist, and my hands maybe two inches from her tits. I prayed she wouldn't move back and touch me between my legs as I knew I'd come into my Skants.

We drove from Brixton to Clapham. She lived in a room in a house in a back street. In those days, whole streets of houses were bedsits. They had been converted from single tenancy to multi in the forties and fifties, and that's how they still were in the late sixties. In those days no one in their right mind wanted to live in Clapham. Now of course lots of people do and they've been converted back again. Everything changes. Nothing stays the same. *That* is the only rule.

Her room was in a three-storey mid-terrace. As we turned the corner into her street I saw two big travel-stained touring bikes, chopped into hogs, parked up, and my erection subsided. There were two dirty road gypsies sitting on her front wall waiting for her. They were back from grape picking in France and needed a doss for the night. We went upstairs and they brought out the wine and dope, and I had tea and felt about twelve years old, and a load of other people from the house joined us.

The two bikers sat next to each other on the floor leaning back against the wall. They had long black dirty hair, loads of stubble and earrings. One wore a black vest and stiff black leather trousers and boots, and the other wore a greasy blue denim shirt and jeans with a leather waistcoat. It was a warm evening and as the sun went down it struck through the window, and the room heated up, and the smoke from the joints that hung in the air made me dizzy. It was obvious that now the bikers had turned up, I wasn't wanted, but I hung around anyway.

About eight o'clock, the biker with the waistcoat went into his rucksack and pulled out a small box. The pair of them laughed about getting it through customs. The one in the vest took out a bent spoon, burnt black on the bottom, and put some water and pale powder into it. He stirred it and lit his lighter and heated the bottom of the spoon. The liquid bubbled and he added more water. The other biker took out a syringe and sucked up the liquid. Meanwhile the first guy took off his belt and wrapped it around his upper arm. His biceps bulged and the veins were dotted with needle marks. His buddy did the business for him. He tapped the needle to get rid of any bubbles, then inserted it into a vein and pushed down the plunger, then quickly pulled a mixture of blood and smack into the glass barrel of the syringe and zapped it back into the vein. The first guy's eyes bulged and almost immediately his nose started to run. He left the needle in his arm and the syringe hung down like an obscene exclamation mark.

I left before I threw up. I got lost in the back streets of Clapham, but I didn't care. Eventually I found my way to the common and sat and watched the sun disappear behind the trees, and shivered as the evening turned to night and the common turned from green to black. I hated her that night. I felt she'd taken the piss. I don't think I ever saw her again, or if I did I ignored her. That's the way I was then. Stupid. She wouldn't even have noticed, I know that now.

Funny thing is, for the life of me I can't remember her name. But I've hated needles ever since that day.

By this time Ninotchka was floating herself. I sat on the edge of the bed and she held my hand. She rambled on about Christ knows what as time passed.

I smoked cigarette after cigarette and our skin stuck together with sweat.

There were one or two people I wanted to see, and one or two questions I wanted answering, but I wasn't going to leave her. So I just sat and smoked, and watched the smoke from my cigarettes vanish like dreams into the shadows at the corner of the room.

13

Ninotchka finally fell asleep about two in the morning. I rolled back her eyelids. The pupils of her eyes looked OK and she was breathing steadily. Her colour was good and she had a strong, regular pulse. I covered her with the eiderdown and went looking for Don. He was still in the hallway outside, sitting on a straight-backed chair looking bored. He stood up when I came out of the suite. 'I want a word with you,' I said.

'Do what?'

'You heard. A serious word.'

'What about?'

'You know.'

'No,' he said.

I walked towards him, and he flexed his muscles. I was so angry I could easily have ended up getting seriously hurt. Then we both heard running footsteps coming from the front of the hotel, muffled by the thick carpet on the floor, and turned and looked in that direction. Roger Lomax came round the corner, skidded slightly, righted himself, then saw us. 'Christ, Sharman!' he said. 'Thank God I've found you.' He was breathing heavily, and his skin was greenish-white with an unhealthy sheen to it.

'What?' I said, forgetting about Don.

'Come with me,' gasped Lomax. Really gasped, like his mouth was dry and his teeth chattering.

'Where?'

'Downstairs. Come on, for God's sake!'

I followed him. We used the stairs, going down two floors to where the roadies had their rooms. Halfway down the hallway a door was open. Outside it, two women were standing together, supporting each other. One of the women had a blonde crop, and was dressed in a short orange dress made of satin and net that looked like a thirties ball gown chopped off mid-thigh. She was leaning against another blonde, but with longer hair, wearing a black mini dress and black tights. Chick and Seltza were with them. They were both looking a little green too. Someone had been sick all over the carpet. It smelled sharp and unpleasant in the heated air.

'Inside,' said Lomax, and nodded at the door. I pushed it all the way open and went inside the room. It was the twin of Seltza's. It contained a dressing table, chest of drawers, table, four upright chairs, two armchairs and a double bed. The window was open and the curtains billowed slightly in the faint breeze from outside.

Turdo lay on the bed. He was flat on his back. His head was twisted to one side. The skin of his face was black. His eyes were bulging out of their sockets, and his tongue jutted out from between lips the colour of liver. Round his neck, drawn tight, was a long length of silver wire. But that wasn't all. There was blood all over his shirt, and underneath him it had soaked into the bedclothes. Protruding from his chest was a stake of varnished light wood with white printing running up its length. It stuck out about four inches from the entry wound and the top had been battered with a hammer or mallet or something similar. The room stank of blood and shit, which combined with the smell of vomit made me want to throw up too. Nevertheless, I went over to Turdo and felt for a pulse, even though I knew I was wasting my time. There was nothing, and his skin was cool. I looked around, Lomax was standing in the doorway. His complexion hadn't improved.

'What the fuck is that?' I said, pointing at Turdo's chest.

'A drumstick,' replied Lomax. 'One of the biggest ones made. A 2B.'

'I don't believe this shit,' I said. 'A fucking drumstick! Are you serious?'

I went to the window. Turdo's room was at the back of the hotel and opened on to a metal fire escape that went down to a paved yard enclosed by iron railings. There was no one in sight. Some security, I thought.

I pushed Lomax out of the door. 'Tell me about it.'

'Turdo called up his girlfriend Jane,' he said. I guessed she was the one in orange. It didn't really matter. Not then. She had started to sob, and there was an edge of hysteria to the sound. 'She was out. He left a message on her machine to come over when she got home. She was at a club with Maddy. They got back late. She got the message. They got a cab over. They met Chick and Seltza at the front door. They came up together. The door was unlocked. They found him like that. Seltza came and got me.'

'Have you called the police?'

Lomax looked at me.

'And don't say no police,' I said. 'This time, police. And get them out of the hall, for Christ's sake. Seltza, take them to your room. Get them a drink or something.'

He nodded, and whispered something to the woman in the black dress who led her friend away in the direction of his room. Lomax made as if to follow them.

'Wait a minute,' I said. 'Before you call, get the rest of your guys knocking on doors. Get everything but prescription drugs off the premises. The coppers will toss this place from top to bottom. Get them to flush the stuff, not the wraps, down the toilet. The Old Bill will have someone check the drains, just to see what they can find.'

'And the wraps?'

'If they're plastic, cut them into strips and then flush them. If they're paper, burn them and flush the ashes. And no fucking around. You don't want anything found on the premises. That goes for everyone, right?'

'Sure.'

'That includes the band and any dealers who happen to be hanging around tonight. And no messing around. This place must be clean.

No stashing. The dogs'll be in by dawn if the police think there's anything tasty hidden here. They probably will anyway. And another thing – make sure Pandora's playmates are in their own room. And try and put a stop to any other deviant behaviour.' I slapped my forehead. 'Oh, Christ!' I said.

'What?'

I pulled him back out of earshot of the others. 'Ninotchka,' I said. 'She's upstairs sleeping off a couple of syringes full of smack. Now why the fuck didn't you tell me?'

'What?'

'What?' I mimicked. 'Shapiro's spiked with smack. Ninotchka hates Shapiro. Ninotchka mainlines smack. A simple equation. One plus one plus one equals three.'

'Now listen...'

'Now listen, nothing!' I interrupted. 'You should have told me.'

'I couldn't,' said Lomax. 'We were together for two years when I first started with the band. She built me up, and built me up. Just like she's been doing to you and a hundred others over the past ten years. Then she dropped me. Bang!' He seemed to be recovering from his earlier panic. 'But I still rate her, OK? And I wasn't about to tell you anything about her. I warned you once, then I decided to let you find out for yourself.'

'Cheers. Who supplies her?'

'Guy called Elmo.'

'Not Sandy?'

'No. Sandy's blow and uppers. Elmo's smack and downers.'

'Jesus, it's like a department store around here,' I said.

He shrugged.

'OK, get started. And get the police quickly. We don't want any suspicious gaps in the story.'

'I'm gone,' he said, and walked off down the corridor after the two roadies and the women.

14

The police arrived with all the subtlety of a tower block being demolished.

They came by the car- and van-load, uniformed and plain clothes, and cordoned off the square, the tunnel leading to the car park, the mews, all entrances to the hotel, and cleared the first floor. I was half expecting a couple of helicopters complete with Krieg lights to hover overhead and bathe the place in their million candlepower beams.

By three a.m. the hotel was thick with Old Bill. Chick, Seltza and I, being the last to see Turdo alive, had been separated and were waiting to be questioned.

I was put in the hotel manager's sitting room with a uniformed constable who looked like a health freak and didn't like me smoking. I waited for an hour and five cigarettes before I was attended to.

Two men in suits came into the room and dismissed the constable. One was thirty-five or so in a dark grey double-breasted number and dirty shoes. His hair was greasy and black and not sure whether it was getting long or not. He had the face of someone who'd got a ticket but missed the boat. The other guy was fiftyish, wearing a single-breasted navy blue whistle with waistcoat. His shoes sparkled and his greying hair was cut short. He, on the other hand, looked like someone who always ended up in first class. Ticket or not.

'Carpenter,' he announced when the uniform had gone. 'Chief

Superintendent. This is my colleague, Detective Inspector Ripley. You're Sharman.'

It was most reassuring to be told. 'What a relief,' I said.

'I beg your pardon?' said Carpenter.

'Nothing,' I said. 'It's just late, you know?'

'I'm well aware of the time, Mr Sharman,' said Carpenter. I had a feeling that this geezer knew exactly who I was.

'Any chance of a cuppa?' I asked.

'Get some tea in, Mike, will you?' said Carpenter.

Ripley looked pained, went to the door, opened it, bellowed 'Tea', closed it again and rejoined his guv'nor.

'Thanks,' I said.

Ripley pulled two straight-backed chairs close up to the sofa where I was sitting and he and Carpenter sat down in front of me. Ripley produced a notebook and a cheap pen. I sat where I was and looked up at them.

'Tell me about tonight,' said Carpenter.

I told him. Ripley took notes. The only bits I left out were those concerning illegal substances. Halfway through the story the telephone on the table rang. Ripley answered. He covered the mouthpiece and said: 'Indian, China or Earl Grey?'

Carpenter looked like he'd swallowed a grapefruit whole. 'Tell them just tea,' he said.

'Indian for me,' I said.

'Indian,' said Ripley and put down the receiver.

I finished the story.

'So the last time you saw Duane Tucker was at approximately nine p.m.?' said Carpenter when I'd finished.

I assumed that Duane Tucker was Turdo. But I checked. Never assume. It can get you into serious trouble. I was right. I agreed that Carpenter's statement was true.

'And he was going to call his girlfriend, Miss Hillman?'

'I don't know her name,' I said. 'But he *was* going to call his girlfriend, that's right.'

'And you never saw him again?'

'Not alive.'

'And you spent the rest of the evening with Miss Landry?'

'Ninotchka,' I said.

He nodded.

'Not all evening,' I said. 'I didn't get to her suite until after ten.'

'And before?'

'I had a drink with the roadies and then went upstairs.'

'To your room?'

'That's right.'

'Alone?'

'Correct.'

'How long had you known Tucker?'

'A few hours, that's all.'

'And the other two members of the entourage, Wallace and Feldman?'

This name business was getting confusing. It turned out that Wallace was Chick and Feldman was Seltza. 'The same,' I said. 'I met all three earlier.'

'And what did they do when you went upstairs?'

'They said they were going out. To see a band at The Astoria.'

'Charing Cross Road,' explained Ripley.

Carpenter nodded.

'So what exactly are you doing here, Mr Sharman?' he asked. 'You're a bit out of your area aren't you?'

Then I knew he knew me. 'I didn't think I needed a passport to cross the river.'

Carpenter gave me a dirty look and the tea arrived. It was served by one of Jones' staff accompanied by another uniformed constable – presumably to make sure the waiter didn't slip us a Mickey in with the plate of assorted biscuits. The tea came in bone china on a silver tray. Not like the usual brew-up in the interview room, I thought.

'That's one reason,' I said. 'Room service.'

'Any others?'

'A job,' I said.

'What kind of job?'

'Security,' I said. 'I was recommended.'

'By?'

'An old client.'

'Does the client have a name, pray?'

'McBain,' I said. 'Mark McBain.'

'Of course. Why exactly?'

'They thought they needed it.'

'It appears they were correct,' said Carpenter dryly.

'It was a hell of a thing,' I said. 'Like some sort of vampire film.'

Carpenter looked at me. It was then that he was going to act like a human being and open up to me, or else play the hard man.

'Unusual,' he said.

'To say the least. What was that round his neck?'

'A guitar string. That's what killed him. Someone used it as a garrotte. Then he was laid out on the bed and that stake thing hammered through his chest. It went right through him and pinned the body to the mattress.'

'It was a drumstick.'

'How did you know that?'

'Roger Lomax recognised it and told me.'

'It must be nice to be musical,' said Carpenter.

I ignored the joke.

'It was sharpened to a point,' he went on.

'Pretty strange,' I said.

'These are strange days. And strange people.'

'But even so. What time did it happen?'

'Should I be telling you?'

'Probably not, but someone will sooner or later, or I'll read it in the papers. I'm sure they're more than interested.'

'Vermin!' said Carpenter. 'They're out there now, baying like hounds.' He was beginning to mix his metaphors, but it was late and who was I to complain. 'It happened about eleven-thirty.'

'I thought so. There were early signs of rigor in the body when I touched it.'

'So you've got an alibi.'

'Do I need one? I'd just had dinner and a few drinks with the man. Christ, we'd just met. I don't usually strangle people and hammer a stake through them until I've known them at least a month.'

Before Carpenter could reply, we were interrupted by a knock on the door. He looked annoyed. Ripley got up and answered it. I saw a uniform outside. Ripley and the owner of the uniform whispered for a minute or so, and Ripley took something from the uniform, then closed the door and came back and handed what he'd taken to Carpenter. He looked at it, smiled sourly and handed it back to Ripley. 'Your solicitor's here,' he said to me.

'My solicitor doesn't know where I am.'

Ripley handed what he'd been given to me. It was a large, thick, cream-coloured business card. Not the sort you get from mini-cab firms and tear up to make roaches. It had to be large to accommodate the dozen or so names of the partners engraved on it in black copperplate. Even I recognised the name of the firm. It was so old that Lincoln's Inn probably had still been fields when they first hung their sign out, and so establishment that if the Prime Minister ever got a pull, they'd be the first number he called. I looked at the card, and when I looked up, Carpenter and Ripley were looking at me.

'Big guns,' said Carpenter.

'As big as you can get before going nuclear,' I replied.

'Not your usual firm, I dare say?' he said. He gave me the impression that he thought my usual firm was some shady sort of brief close to disbarment who carried his office around in his hat. He wasn't far wrong.

'No,' I replied.

'Well, I think we'll wrap this up for now,' said Carpenter to Ripley. 'And let Mr Sharman consult his brief, and then get some sleep. I'm sure we don't want to be accused of harassment, especially by a representative of such an eminent firm.' Then to me: 'Will you make yourself available in the morning?'

'Don't leave town?' I said.

'Don't leave the building,' said Carpenter. And he and Ripley got up and left the room.

15

I sat on the sofa for a minute or two more, then got up and left the room myself. It was bloody late or bloody early, depending on which way you liked to look at it, but the young man standing in the hallway was as immaculate as if he'd had a good night's sleep, a shave, shower, and plenty of time to co-ordinate the outfit he was wearing.

He was dressed in a black suit, cut tight, with a flowered waistcoat, a dark green shirt with a stiff white collar, a flowered tie that matched the waistcoat, and highly polished, pointy-toed black shoes. A white silk handkerchief flopped out of his breast pocket. His hair was short, perfectly cut, with a knife-edged parting on the right-hand side. In his left hand he was holding a black leather briefcase with gold fittings. He was so neat I was tempted to look for the polythene bag he came in.

'Mr Sharman?' he said, and stuck out his right hand. 'James Prendegast at your service.'

I looked at the card I was still holding. James Prendegast was listed as one of the partners. 'My new brief?' I said.

'In one.'

I shook his hand. His grip was firm and warm and reassuring.

'Courtesy of the band, I assume?'

'Right again. It's a pleasure to meet you.'

'The feeling's mutual,' I said. 'You must be pretty scary. You certainly got those coppers off my back in double quick time.'

'Sometimes the mere mention of the old firm has that effect.' He laughed. 'But I'm afraid I'm rather sailing under false colours. The James Prendegast on the card is my father. I'm just a junior in more ways than one, and I'm not alone here tonight. One or two of the partners are dotted around the place. I'm afraid you rather got the booby prize.'

'Better than no prize at all,' I said. 'And you seemed to have the required effect.'

'That's an admirable attitude, I must say. Can we go to your suite? I'd like a little chat.'

'It's very late,' I said.

'I won't keep you long, I promise. Just a few words and I'll pop along.'

'Come on then,' I said, and we went towards the lifts together. We met Wilfred in the hallway outside my door. He was full of questions about what had happened and stories about being accosted by journalists on his way to work and then getting through the police lines to get into the hotel. 'I've got my breakfasts to cook, I told them,' he said. 'I've never missed getting the breakfasts in eleven years and I'm not about to start now.' He had some late editions of the tabloids with the story of Turdo's murder splashed all over the front page. I relieved him of a couple of them and he promised fresh coffee in less than five minutes.

'Brilliant, Wilfred,' I said. 'I don't know what we'd do without you.'

'Drink Perrier, sir,' he said. 'I'll be with you directly.'

I let Prendegast Jr into my suite and he sat down at the table and took a notebook out of his briefcase and a huge black and gold Mont Blanc fountain pen out of his breast pocket. I sat on the sofa.

'Well, Mr Sharman,' he said. 'It seems as if we have a few problems.'

'We?'

'The ancillaries to *Pandora's Box*.'

'Well, that's one way of describing me, I suppose,' I said. 'I've heard worse.'

He smiled again. 'Do you intend to stay?'

'Stay?'

'Do you intend to continue with your employment?'

'I've come this far.'

'Splendid. I think they're going to need someone like you around over the next few days.'

'They'd probably do better with someone like you. I don't make big strong coppers vanish at the mere mention of my name. Just the opposite, in fact.'

'Ah, but you have other qualities.'

'Right now I wouldn't like to have to list them,' I said. There was a knock on the door. I went and opened it. Wilfred was outside carrying a steaming coffee pot, cups, milk and sugar on a tray. I held the door open for him. He put the tray on the table and poured us a cup each. 'Thanks, Wilfred,' I said wearily.

'I take it you've had no sleep, sir?'

'No.'

'Do you intend going to bed?'

'No.'

'Then these may help.' And he took two turquoise and grey capsules from his waistcoat pocket.

'Are those what I think they are?'

'Amphetamine, sir,' he said. 'I find them invaluable after a late night and an early start.'

'You amaze me, Wilfred. Are they street legal?'

'Perfectly, sir. I have a prescription from my medico.'

I took them from him. 'Well, here goes nothing,' I said. 'What's a little more speed on an empty stomach?' And I swallowed the pair of them and washed them down with a mouthful of coffee. Prendegast Jr watched the whole transaction without a word. Wilfred left with a wink and I sat down on the sofa again with the remains of my coffee.

'Tell me what happened last night?' said Prendegast Jr.

So I told him as the speed kicked in and I began to feel better.

We finished the pot as I talked. Prendegast Jr was pretty non-committal. Before he left, just as seven o'clock struck, he asked me to call him if I came across or remembered anything relevant. I agreed to do so. 'Stir up the place,' he said as he stood at the door. 'You're pretty good at that, I believe. I'll keep in touch.' And we shook hands again.

After he'd left I took a shower, shaved, put on clean clothes and took a wander to see what I could see.

16

I went down to the restaurant on the ground floor. Although it was early, it was crowded with road crew and the sort of ancillaries to *Pandora's Box* that Prendegast Jr had referred to. It was almost as if they were huddled together for comfort. Even though the room was full, it was strangely silent, and no one seemed to be doing much eating. Instead there were whispered conversations at each table, and much coffee and many cigarettes were being consumed. There were no band members present. I saw Chick and Seltza at a corner table with Chippy. I went over.

Chippy looked up and saw me coming. 'Fucking Magnum PI,' he said as I got to the table. Seltza shushed him. All three roadies were white-faced and looked angry. 'Hi, Nick,' said Seltza. 'Bad morning, yeah?'

'Yeah,' I agreed.

'Sit down, buddy,' he said. 'Want something to eat?'

I didn't feel hungry, but I thought I might be able to chase some scrambled egg around a plate. The waiter took my order when he arrived with two pots of freshly brewed coffee for the table. I helped myself to a cup and one of Seltza's cigarettes.

'Did you guys get any sleep?' I asked.

'No, man,' said Chick. 'It wasn't that kind of night.'

'How long were you with the police?' I asked.

'Too long,' answered Seltza. 'But then some British attorney showed up and the cops let me go. You?'

'The same.'

'Me too,' said Chick. 'There's gotta be some advantages to working for a rich band.'

'Yeah,' said Chippy. 'You can end up getting murdered for a grand and a half a week plus exes. I'd rather work for a poor band and stay healthy.'

The other two nodded as if in agreement.

'Shit, man,' said Seltza, 'I'd like to get my hands on whoever did that to Turdo. We go back a long way. A long, long way.' There was nothing for me to add to that. We all suffer our losses, and we all have to cope with them the best we can. 'Have you seen the papers?' he asked.

'Briefly,' I replied. 'They're having a field day.'

'They're loving every minute of my buddy getting killed,' he said bitterly. 'There's a whole bunch of reporters outside. The English press. Man, they're shit! If I bump into one of them down a dark alley, they'll wish I hadn't.'

There was nothing for me to add to that either. 'It sells,' was all I could think of.

'Who do you think did it?' asked Seltza after a minute.

'God knows,' I replied. 'You got there before me. What do you think?'

'I think there's a real crazy running around this hotel. I don't like it, man.'

'What are you going to do about it?' I asked.

He narrowed his eyes and looked at me, and I wished I hadn't.

'You mean am I going to quit?' he asked quietly.

'That's about it.'

'No, man. I signed on for the duration. Win, lose or draw. If some fucker wants to see me out of here, he's not going to get the satisfaction, whoever he is.' The other two mumbled their agreement.

'Good,' I said.

The waiter arrived with my order, but the sight and smell of the eggs made me feel vaguely nauseous and I pushed the plate away. I poured a second cup of coffee and lit another of Seltza's Malboros.

At that point Prendegast Jr came into the room. He looked round, then made for our table. 'Gentlemen,' he said, 'the police are here again. They have a few more questions, and they want to take a simple statement from each of you. Naturally you will all have a solicitor present throughout. There's nothing to worry about. I've been asked to liaise with the police as well as acting for Mr Sharman. The statements are being taken in the snooker room in the basement.'

'Just us?' I asked.

'I'm sorry.'

'Are we the only ones being questioned?'

'No, no, no. Everyone in the hotel is being interviewed. But the police are particularly interested in the people who were present when the body was found and directly after.'

'What happened to Jane and Maddy?' asked Seltza.

'They were found accommodation here. The hotel doctor put Miss Hillman under sedation. The police will talk to them later.'

'When do they want to see me?' I asked.

'When do you want to see them?'

'I'd like to see Ninotchka first.'

He didn't ask me why. I liked that. It showed trust, and a certain healthy respect for one of the people who'd ultimately be paying his fee. 'Go and see her then,' he said. 'The police are being very co-operative. This is an extremely delicate case. They're handling it with the proverbial kid gloves.'

'You mean there's rich and famous people involved, and the newspapers are beating the doors down?' I said.

'Believe me, it's an advantage. It keeps everything legal and above board. I'm sure we wouldn't want it any other way.'

I was sure too. I'd seen a few cases that hadn't been and I hadn't liked them. 'Have they got any leads?' I asked.

'None that they're prepared to share with me. Now you'd better go if you're going, and go that way.' He gestured towards the kitchen. 'There are a couple of uniformed officers outside. I don't want them to see you before you're prepared to be seen.'

I did as he suggested. I went into the kitchen, and after a quiet word with the waiter who'd served me earlier, through the staff quarters and up the back stairs to the top floor of the hotel and Ninotchka's suite.

On the landing inside the connecting door between the staircase and the corridor were two Premiere security men. They must have heard me coming up. It wouldn't have been difficult. It was a long climb and I'm not as fit as I should be. They were both standing in the shadows, and both held Smith & Wesson Model 38 Bodyguard Air-weight revolvers. After a bit you get to notice things like that. 'Come up slowly,' said the smaller of the pair. 'And let us see your hands are empty.'

I climbed the last few stairs, holding my hands well clear of my body. I recognised them as the pair who'd been in the entrance to the lift two days before to check me in.

'Easy,' I said. 'Remember me, Ronnie?'

'Mr Sharman, isn't it?' he said, lowering his gun.

'That's right. I want to see Ninotchka.'

'Why use the back stairs?' asked the other, the one who wouldn't speak to me when we were in the lift together. Big Phil. I think my being brought in had hurt his professional pride.

'I didn't want to run into any of the boys in blue until I'd had a chance to talk to her.'

Ronnie nodded as if it were par for the course, and took a radio telephone out of his jacket pocket and pressed the send button. 'Premiere two to Premiere one,' he said.

'Go ahead, Premiere two,' said a metallic voice from the small speaker.

'I've got Mr Sharman here. He wants to see Ninotchka. OK to let him through?'

There was a pause. 'Premiere two from Premiere one. Mr Sharman has access all areas. Escort him to her suite.'

'Roger Roj,' said Ronnie and put the R/T away. 'I'll walk you through, sir,' he said. 'We've drafted in extra boys this morning and they won't know you. We don't want anyone getting over keen, do we?'

I certainly didn't. Not if they were the calibre of Big Phil and all carried S&Ws.

'I'm obliged,' I said.

There was a Premiere man outside every door. They were all new faces, and I nodded politely to each and every one as I passed them. Outside Ninotchka's suite was another stranger. Ronnie knocked on the door and went in. 'Just checking she's decent,' he said to me. 'Wait here.' I did as I was told.

I looked at the security man and smiled my most pleasant smile. He nodded back. That was us, just two honest men trying to earn a crust in the best way we knew how. 'How many inside?' I asked, nodding towards the door.

'Enough,' he replied.

'Bad business last night.'

'So they say.'

He wasn't giving much away. 'Think it might rain later?'

'Possibly.'

I smiled a wry smile. Even he relaxed a little and showed his gums when he did.

The door behind him opened and Ronnie reappeared. 'OK, Mac,' he said to the security man. 'She'll see him.'

I stepped past Mac and into the sitting room of the suite. There were two more Premiere employees inside. Their name plates read 'Stan' and 'Hughie'. Stan was a man mountain with a completely shaven head and a track suit. Hughie had bright red hair and the look of a Scottish football hooligan.

'She said for you to wait in there,' said Stan, and pointed to the door of the bedroom that had been converted into an office.

I nodded to Ronnie, and went in, and sat on the edge of the desk and lit a cigarette.

Ninotchka joined me a few minutes later and closed the door behind her. She looked fine. 'Hello,' she said. I could hear a certain coolness in her voice I hadn't heard before. I wondered if this was the start of the famous Ninotchka freeze out. What the hell? If it was, it was.

'Why didn't you tell me?' I asked.

'What?'

'That you're strung out on horse. What else?'

'It was none of your business.'

'Come on, Ninotchka, don't give me that,' I said.

'It wasn't.'

'Yes, it was, under the circumstances. I thought you trusted me?'

'I did. I do.'

'Then why not tell me?'

She shrugged, but didn't elaborate further. The silence hung there like a shroud. 'So what now?' she asked eventually. Then it was my turn to shrug at her, and we were both silent again.

She found a cigarette in a packet on the desk and made a big production out of lighting it. She blew out a stream of grey smoke through her teeth with a hiss. 'Talking of trust,' she said, 'Roger tells me you think I might be involved with Trash's OD.'

'I never said that. What I said was that the police might think you were, if they knew what you were up to last night. One thing I do know – if whoever killed Turdo is the same one who tried to kill Shapiro, then it wasn't you. When it happened you were right here with me. Unless you've got accomplices and you're a very cool operator indeed. In fact, I know for sure of only two people who didn't do it. You and me.'

At that, she seem to relax visibly, stubbed out the cigarette in an ashtray and came to me, and we held each other tightly. It was good to feel some human contact. 'Thank God,' she said. 'I thought from what Roger said…'

'No,' I interrupted. 'Roger was a bit freaked last night. We all were.'

'Was it awful?'

'I've seen worse, but not often.' I didn't really want to think about it.

'Did you speak to the police yet?' she asked.

'Last night for a while.'

'They want to see me later.'

'They want to see me now. Just make sure you've got a brief with you.'

'A what?'

'An attorney.'

'Oh, yeah, sure.'

'Your people have brought in a first-class firm. The best. Even the cops are shit scared of them. Now the only thing you've got to be worried about is any drugs you've got stashed away here.'

'Roger came up last night and disposed of what was left. That's the trouble.'

'What?'

'I've got to get more.'

'*Ninotchka*,' I said.

'I need it.'

'For Christ's sake!'

'What the fuck do you know?'

'OK,' I said, holding my hands up in surrender. 'So get more.'

'How the hell am I going to do that with the police all over the place?'

'You're not in prison,' I said. 'You will be allowed out later.'

'Have you seen what it's like outside? It's a zoo. The press are everywhere.'

'What about Don?'

'He won't. I asked him before he went off duty. He says it's more than his job's worth.' I had to smile at that.

The ultimate excuse of the small-minded. 'Will you?' she asked.

'Me?'

'All you have to do is pick up a parcel. It's already been arranged.'

'From Elmo?'

She nodded.

'That was quick.'

She nodded again.

If she expected me to argue, she was going to be disappointed. That was fine by me. He was just the man I wanted to speak to.

'OK, Ninotchka,' I said.

'You will? Nick, you're a treasure.'

'No problem. When?'

'Later this afternoon.'

'As long as I'm through with the cops,' I said. 'I've only got to make a short statement. I tell them I was with you. You do the same. Now I'd better go and do it.'

She kissed me on the cheek and I left. I smiled politely to the heavy mob in the sitting room. Ninotchka told them to let me in any time night or day. I think I went up in their estimation at that.

I went looking for Prendegast Jr and the luminaries of the law.

I found a clutch of uniformed coppers outside the snooker room. 'My name's Sharman,' I said to a uniformed sergeant. 'I believe Mr Carpenter is looking for me?'

'If you'll wait he'll see you soon,' he replied.

I sat on one of the upright chairs that had been lined up against the wall and waited. Chick came out with a dapper middle-aged man in a charcoal grey suit. I'd never seen him before.

'Hi, Nick,' said Chick. 'Meet Mr Sebastian, my solicitor.' I stood up and we shook hands. 'I hope young Prendegast is looking after you?' said Sebastian.

'Yes,' I replied.

'Good. As I told Mr Wallace here, you don't have a thing to worry about.'

'That's nice,' I said. 'But I'm not sure my bank manager would agree.'

Sebastian chuckled, the kind of dry chuckle that people do when they don't share your sense of humour, know you've made a joke, but don't quite understand the point of it. Looking at him, I would have bet he'd never had trouble with a bank manager in his life. He probably played golf with his. 'Splendid,' he said, which covered a multitude of sins, and Prendegast Jr came out of the snooker room, excused himself to Sebastian, grabbed me, and wheeled me in. A big snooker table that I assumed usually stood under the low, oblong, green metal lampshade that hung down from the ceiling, had been covered and pushed into one corner. A desk had been set up and Carpenter and Ripley were sitting behind it facing the door. Two uncomfortable-looking upright chairs covered with green velvet, with curved, polished wooden arms, stood this side of the desk. At a smaller table next to the desk sat a uniformed constable in shirtsleeve order holding a pen and a shorthand notebook. On the desk in front of him was an electric typewriter and a pile of clean A4-sized paper.

'Mr Sharman,' said Carpenter quite pleasantly, 'thank you for giving us your time.' My God, I thought, he *is* being friendly. I wondered when the catch would show itself. 'Please be seated,' he went on. 'The constable here will take down your statement, type it up for your signature, and then you are free to go. Is that acceptable?'

I looked at Prendegast Jr. It seemed fair enough to me, but I was still waiting for the catch and wanted to be sure. He nodded, and who was I to argue? I nodded too and we both sat down.

I ran through the events of the previous evening from the time I first met Turdo until the police arrived. Once again I left out only the drug references. The evening must have sounded like a vicarage tea party. The uniform took it down and then machine gunned on the typewriter. I read the finished statement, signed each page and left. Simple as that.

Outside Prendegast Jr said, 'No pain?'

'None at all,' I replied. 'Except for the poor bastard that got topped. The police don't actually seem to be doing much.'

'Believe me, they are,' he said. 'They've set up an incident room next door in the tennis court, and are making themselves very busy indeed. This is just the tip of the iceberg.' He looked at his watch and frowned. 'I'm going to have to leave you now,' he said, 'but I'll be around the hotel. Please keep in touch.'

'I will,' I said. We shook hands and parted. I went up to my suite. By then it was almost ten o'clock, and I had an eleven o'clock appointment with Keith Pandora that I didn't want to miss.

17

That's right. You guessed it. Outside Pandora's suite was yet another plug ugly in a grey suit with a badge on his lapel. The whole place was crawling with them. As I walked up to the door he stepped forward and put up his left hand like a policeman stopping traffic. He let his right hand hover near the front of his open jacket. 'Hold your fire,' I said. 'I come in peace.'

'What?'

'Nothing. I'm here to see Keith Pandora. I've got an appointment. My name's Sharman.'

'What do you want to see him about?'

'That's my business.' These guys were getting as officious as hell. Anyone would think they were Old Bill themselves. The security man just stood there, hand still upheld like a wax work. 'Go on then,' I said. 'Tell him.'

His hand moved closer to the front of his suit jacket. 'Smith & Wesson hammerless, isn't it?' I said. And his hand stopped dead. He didn't answer. 'Got a radio?' I asked.

'What if I have?'

'Cut the crap, will you? Call your control. They'll tell you I'm OK.'

'What the fuck?' he said, and knocked on the door. It opened almost immediately. 'Bloke called Sharman,' said the guard out of the corner of his mouth, never taking his eyes off me.

There was silence from the other side of the door.

We waited for a minute or two, then: 'Yo,' said a voice inside. 'Let him come ahead.'

The guard stepped out of my way and I went inside. The room was lit only by artificial light. All the curtains were drawn tight. There were another two security men present. One was sitting on one of the sofas. The other stood inside the doorway. He was in shirtsleeves. Around his waist, slung horizontally above his left-hand trouser pocket, was a black leather holster housing his S&W in a cross draw position. 'The guv'nor's not up yet,' he said.

'I'll wait.'

'I would if I was you. He likes people to wait for him.'

'How long do you reckon?' I asked.

'Dunno.'

'Are we talking minutes, hours, days? Have I got time for lunch or a jog around Hyde Park?'

'Dunno,' he said again. 'What does it matter? You got something else better to do?'

'No,' I said.

'Sit down then. He'll be along when he's ready.'

I went over to an armchair and took a seat. I pulled out my cigarettes and lit one. The room was very quiet. If I'd've had a pin handy I'd've dropped it to break the silence. I smoked the cigarette and then another. The hands on the face of my watch crept round to 11.20. Then the door to one of the bedrooms crashed open and Keith Pandora burst into the room.

'Mornin', chaps,' he said in an exaggerated cockney accent.

The two security men replied 'Mornin'' in unison. I just looked at him. His hair was like a lion's mane. Various shades of blond curls hung around the shoulders of his blue paisley silk dressing gown. It was open to the waist and I could see greying hair tufted on his bony chest. The dressing gown stopped just above his knees. His legs were thin, but muscular and tanned. 'I fancy a game of tennis later,' he said. 'I think I'll get on the court after lunch.'

'I think the police have taken it over for their incident room.'

'Oh, Christ! What a drag. Do you think I can get a game somewhere else?'

I wondered who he thought I was. The chairman of the British Lawn Tennis Association maybe? 'No idea,' I said. 'Sport bores me.'

He looked at me like I'd just hatched out of an egg.

'How very interesting,' he said.

'Not as interesting as murder,' I said. 'But you obviously don't think so.'

'You sound like the voice of my conscience.'

I didn't answer. The two security men looked on like the trained monkeys they were.

'Well?' he demanded.

'Maybe.'

'And what gives you the right to tell me what I'm interested in or not?'

I shrugged. 'I thought you might be interested when one of your guys gets killed.'

He looked at me long and hard. 'Do you know who you're talking to?' he asked.

'Yeah,' I said. 'I know.'

'Then don't tell me about my guys. My guys get very well paid for what they do. You should know that. You're not doing too badly yourself. If something happens to them that's their lookout. And yours.'

'You're a sweetheart, do you know that?'

'I'll make a note of it. But remember one thing – this is a rock and roll band, not a bunch of poofs on a church outing. We've lost people before, and I guess we will again. And when we do, we close ranks. We don't cry over spilt milk. We party. It might be me next time, and I don't want any fucking mourning done on my behalf. That's the way my guys are too. Turdo was OK. Now he's gone. We'll all remember him with love, we'll take care of any arrangements that have to be made, but life goes on. That's one thing you learn in this business. Now you two,' he looked at the security men, 'I want you to get lost. Me and Nick here've got things to talk about in private.'

I thought they might protest, but he just gave them a dirty look and they didn't argue. 'And where the hell's my breakfast?' he added.

As if on cue there was a knock on the door. The guy in shirtsleeves put his hand on the butt of his pistol and opened it a crack, then all the way, and a Jones' waiter came in wheeling a trolley piled with covered dishes. 'Great,' said Pandora. The waiter covered the dining table with a clean white cloth and transferred the dishes on to it, taking off the covers as he went, and putting them back on to the trolley. Then he bowed out, like he'd been delivering breakfast to Prince Charles.

'OK,' said Pandora. 'You two can split and leave us alone.'

'Sure, Mr Pandora,' said the one in shirtsleeves and picked up his jacket and put it on. 'We'll be right outside. Just yell if you need us.'

'I'm safe with Nick here,' said Pandora.

The two men nodded and left. Pandora sat at the table and loaded the plate in front of him with food. He was no mean eater. He chose scrambled eggs, bacon, two kinds of sausage, kidneys, kedgeree and hot rolls. The smell of the food made me feel slightly sick again. 'Want some?' he said with his mouth full of egg.

I shook my head in reply.

'Coffee?'

'Sure.' I stood up, walked to the table and poured black coffee into a clean cup and added cream and sugar, then went back to my chair.

'Well, Nick,' said Pandora. 'It seems that bringing you in didn't work out like we'd planned it.'

'Or extra security men,' I replied.

'True.' He hesitated. 'Are you making excuses for yourself?'

I shook my head. 'No. I was called in to investigate a possible attempted murder. Now there's been a real one. Someone moved the goalposts. Changed the rules. We're talking a whole different ballgame.'

He pursed his lips. 'You saw Turdo's body?'

I nodded. 'It was rough,' I said. 'Whoever did that must have been crazy. And tough. He was a big man.'

It was Pandora's turn to nod.

'But then,' I went on, 'your band seems to be pretty unlucky like that.'

'Yeah?'

'Yeah. I heard you've had a lot of bad breaks. Like you said, lost a lot of people over the years.'

'We're not the only ones. This business attracts strange people, and strange things often happen. We've had our share.'

'More than your share if you ask me.'

He didn't answer, just finished the last scraps on his plate and drained his coffee cup and wiped his mouth with his napkin.

'Gotta cigarette?' he asked.

I tossed him the packet and he lit one with a match from a complimentary book advertising the hotel, sat back and blew out a stream of smoke. 'Thanks,' he said. 'I quit.'

'They always taste better after,' I remarked.

'Sure do,' he agreed, then changed the subject. 'Have you met all the band yet?'

'No,' I replied. 'It's been kind of hectic since I got here.'

'Who *have* you met?'

'You. Box. Shapiro. And Ninotchka.'

'Ah, Ninotchka. I've been hearing things about you two. Got your leg over yet?'

'No,' I said. 'If it's any of your business.'

'Everything to do with this band is my business. Still, she's slowing down. She must be getting old.'

He saw my expression.

'Don't get me wrong,' he said, 'I love that woman. If things had been different…' He didn't finish the sentence. 'But they weren't. So you've got to meet Shorty, Baby Boy and Scratch? Listen, tonight we're all getting together for dinner. The lot of us, and Rodge the Dodge. Why don't you come along?'

'Fine,' I said.

'Nine o'clock in the restaurant downstairs. Then we're going on…' The ringing of the telephone interrupted him. He leant over and scooped up the receiver and said: 'Pandora.' He listened for a moment 'Sure,' he said. 'Come on up.' He put down the phone. 'I've got some company coming. I'll get dressed. Won't be long.' He dropped the cigarette into his cup, got up and went back towards the door he'd entered by.

'Want me to go?' I asked.

'No,' he said. 'Stick around.'

He was back within a few minutes. He'd changed into tight white jeans, a Chambray shirt, and dark blue high-topped boat shoes with no socks. Almost immediately there was a knock on the door. He went over and opened it. His two teenaged girlfriends came in. 'Meet Slash and The Flea,' he said. He touched the blonde when he said 'Slash', and the brunette when he said 'The Flea'.

'Hello,' I said. They didn't reply, just looked at me like I was something out of an exhibition. An exhibition that didn't particularly interest them. I wondered if they practised the look in the mirror when they were alone. Pandora closed the door and stood between them, a proprietorial arm around their shoulders. Both the girls were chewing gum. Their jaws moved in unison. Slash was the taller of the two, and her blonde hair was piled up so high on the top of her head she appeared to be even taller than she was. She was dressed all in black. Black jeans, black T-shirt and black trainers. Her lipstick was black too. She looked like she'd been eating licorice. The Flea was wearing a white blouse tucked into a short denim skirt. Underneath the blouse she was wearing a black bra. Subtle.

Pandora left them, and walked to the sofa facing me and sat down. 'Any idea who did it?' he asked.

'Not one.'

He nodded. 'See what you can do.'

'You mean I'm still on the job?'

'Sure. Now tonight there's a big reception –'

'*The Miracle?*'

He nodded. 'You've heard about it. Good. That's where we're going after dinner. All of us. Band, crew, accountants, lawyers. The works. It's a gesture of solidarity. We have to show that we're ready to boogie. To kick ass. Understand? And you're coming too.'

I nodded again.

'Your job is to look out for Ninotchka, OK?'

'Suits me.'

'Don't be coy. I know guys who would kill for the job. Sorry. Not funny, right? Anyway, you might get lucky. Who knows?' And he grinned and showed his big teeth. They were very wet, and very yellow under the artificial light. 'That's settled then,' he said, and looked over at the two sisters. 'Hey, girls, come and sit with me. I'm feeling lonely all of a sudden.'

Slash joined him on the sofa. She sat real close. He draped his right arm over her right shoulder. His hand slid to rest comfortably on the top of her breast. He started rubbing it. Just a lazy rubbing, without really thinking. The pressure brought the nipple up against the material of her T-shirt. And as he stroked her, he was still rabbiting on to me. God knows what about. I wasn't listening. She was looking me straight in the eye as it was going on, as if to get some sort of reaction. It suddenly struck me, clear as day, that they were going through the whole performance for my benefit. To see what I'd do. Then The Flea came over and sat on his left side. He slid his hand down her back, and down further, and she giggled. Then she started squirming around so that I knew his fingers were up her skirt. And I knew they were doing it for my benefit too.

And right then I realised I really hated this guy Pandora. *Really* hated him. And I also realised that as both his hands were otherwise engaged, out of the game as it were, that if I stood up quickly I could drop kick him right in the head and spread that beak of his right across his stupid fucking face. No danger. No problem. Hole in fucking one.

And wouldn't that have been a surprise to the little honey bunnies as they tried to put Humpty together again? Then I realised something else. That I was envious. Which put an entirely new complexion on things.

I stood up, but I didn't kick him. If I had, I'd've lost.

'What's the matter?' he said.

'Nothing. I've got things to do. I'll see you at dinner.'

He grinned like he knew exactly what I was thinking. 'Don't be late.'

18

After I left Pandora's suite, I went looking for Lomax. He was in the bar nursing a Mexican beer and a piece of lime. I ordered similar and took it over to his dimly lit booth. 'How's tricks?'

'Shit,' he said. 'This is just what we didn't want – some of the band are talking about going back to the States.'

'What about the recording?'

'They're saying, fuck it. Pick it up in LA.'

'And lose the release date?'

'And save their lives.'

'I've just been talking to Pandora.'

'Lucky you.'

'You might say that. Personally, I can't stand the fucker.'

'Join the club.'

'Are you sure you should be saying that about the big man?'

'Fuck the big man! I can't stick him either. But I must say, he's been keeping busy since I woke him up at God knows what unearthly hour this morning.'

'Doing what?'

'Organising. He's good at it. Trying to hold the band together.'

'Was he alone?'

'When?'

'When you woke him up?'

'Yeah.'

'No teenyboppers?'

'No, thank Christ. That would have been all I needed. They were safely tucked up in their own beds.'

'I thought not. They turned up a few minutes ago. He seemed to be pretty horny.'

'Did he put on one of his shows for your benefit?'

'How did you know?'

'Christ, I should. He does it for everybody. He thinks it makes him look like stud number one.'

'It makes him look like arsehole number one.'

'You can say that again.'

'I almost altered his face for him.'

'What made you change your mind?'

I didn't answer.

Then I saw the light bulb come on over his head. Just like in a Tom and Jerry cartoon. 'Did it get you hot?' he asked.

'It started to. So I left.'

'You're lucky. Most of us need permission to leave the king's presence.'

'Maybe someone should knock his crown off?'

'Someone's trying.'

'Do you think they'll succeed?'

'After what I saw last night, anything's possible.'

'It was rough.'

'Worse than rough. Turdo was a stand-up guy.'

'Any idea who'd go to those lengths?'

'Shit, I don't know. I'm no detective.'

'I don't seem to be doing too well either.'

'Any ideas?' he asked.

'Everyone asks me that. I haven't got a clue. Nor have the police, according to my brief.'

'How did Keith feel about it this morning? I haven't seen him since daybreak.'

'Mighty fine. He seems convinced that you're all sticking together.'

'He bloody well would be,' said Lomax.

'He wants to stay.'

'He's going to stay. His mother's still sick.'

'He doesn't seem to spend much time with her.'

'He has his moments.'

'I'm sure he does. By the way, I believe we're dining together tonight.'

'Is that so?'

'I got an invite from the boss himself.'

'You're honoured.'

'Then on to a party.'

'*The Miracle's* reception. Should be a hell of a thrash. Any other time and I'd've been looking forward to it.'

'I'm escorting Ninotchka.'

He gave me a funny look. 'Is that so?' he said again.

'It's a dirty job, but someone's got to do it.' He shook his head sorrowfully. Suddenly *I* felt like the arsehole. 'Sorry, pal,' I said. 'Didn't mean it. I'm tired.'

'Aren't we all?'

'Did the coppers put you through it last night?'

'No. Not really. I demanded a phone call and dragged our lawyers out of bed. One mention of their name and the police were very polite.'

'So I noticed. I wish I could afford that kind of muscle on my side all the time.'

'You've got it for the duration. You've been under the corporate umbrella from the moment you signed on.'

'That's reassuring to know. But I wonder how long it's going to last.'

'We'll have a better idea later. I'm going to talk to the crew. Tell them that anyone who wants to split, can. No hard feelings, a flight home, and a month's pay. I can't expect these people to stay here and wonder if they're going to be next for the chop.'

'So he's won?'

'Who?'

'Whoever's behind all this.'

'Looks like it.'

'I think a lot will stay.'

'I hope you're right. Then we might get this album released on time.'

'Are you?'

'What?'

'Staying.'

'Sure. Dependable old Roger. I'll be here 'til my boogie shoes wear out.'

'Even though you can't stand Pandora?'

'Hey, he's not the worst guy in the world to work for. There's plenty make him look like a *real* prince. Man, I could tell you some stories would make your hair curl. I'll survive. And very nicely too. Anyway, he's not the only one in the band. I don't have to see all that much of him if I don't want to. But don't let's talk about it. It's depressing. Are you coming to the meeting?'

I shook my head. 'You can tell me all about it later. At dinner. I've got a few things to do this afternoon.'

'Like?'

'Nothing much. A few errands to run is all.'

He looked at me strangely. 'Be careful.'

'I'm only popping down the shops.' Which I was in a way.

'Don't take any wooden nickels.'

'I'll try and avoid it.'

'OK then.'

I finished my beer. 'Catch you later,' I said, and left.

I wandered down to reception. Always the place in a hotel to catch the gossip. I arrived at the same time as Shapiro arrived back from the hospital. He had Lindy Hopp on his arm, and a pair of Premiere bodyguards with him. They burst through the front entrance to an accompaniment of flash bulbs and shouted questions from the press corps outside. As soon as Shapiro and Lindy were in, the security men blocked the doorway behind them. I ambled over.

'Morning,' I said.

'Jesus!' said Shapiro. 'This place. I wish I'd stayed in hospital.'

'You're not a bad judge,' I said. 'Good morning, Mrs Shapiro.'

'Lindy,' she said, and to my surprise bobbed up and kissed me on the cheek. I took it I was forgiven for upsetting her before.

'What's going on, man?' said Shapiro. 'What the hell happened to Turdo? Jesus, that guy was like one of the band.'

'Not a healthy thing to be right now,' I said.

'He's right Trash,' said Lindy. 'We should split right now.'

'I can't, Lindy. The album…'

'Screw the album!'

'If I do, I screw myself. I spoke to Keith this morning on the telephone. He called me at the hospital. I agreed to stay.'

'I hope you don't regret it. Or me,' she said.

I didn't want to get involved in a domestic. 'Listen, I've got things to do,' I said. 'I'll catch you two later, OK?'

'OK,' said Shapiro. And he and his wife, bodyguards in tow, made for the lift. I took the stairs. I went down to the garage. I always kept a faded old pair of jeans, a battered Avirex leather jacket and a pair of boots in the back of my car. In my game you never know when a change of clothes will come in handy.

19

I went to my suite and changed back into them. If I was going out to score, I at least intended to give some impression of street. True, they were teamed with a mustard-coloured linen shirt whose price tag had bitten a good chunk out of two hundred nicker. But then, who needs street that bad?

Ready for the off, I went up one more flight to Ninotchka's suite. The boys in grey were still in evidence, chillin' out over steak sandwiches and low-alcohol lager for lunch. She gave me a high-alcohol beer from the fridge behind the bar and we went into her office to get some privacy. 'I'd hate to be famous,' I said, lighting a cigarette. 'You've got all this space, but you have to hide in here to talk.'

'One of the penalties of fame,' she said. 'I have to change my phone number every two or three days at home.'

'Yeah?'

'Sure.'

'Strange way to live.'

'You get used to it.'

'I don't know if I could.'

'You had your chance.'

I smiled. 'Yeah, I know.' Then I got serious. 'What's the deal?' I asked.

She knew what I was talking about. 'He's at this address.' She gave me a piece of paper. I looked at it. Smith Street, Chelsea.

'Nice,' I said.

'What did you expect? A cold-water apartment in one of the projects?'

'Come again?'

'You know, public housing. What the hell do you call them over here?'

'Council estates?' I said.

'That's it.'

'I don't know what I expected,' I said. 'Is the gear paid for?'

'It's on my account.'

'Knock three times and ask for Elmo, right?'

'Something like that.'

'Am I expected?'

She nodded.

'By name?'

'Just Nick.'

'I hope everything goes OK.'

'You'll be all right, Nick. You even look like a junkie today.'

Funnily enough, she didn't. 'That's what I'm afraid of,' I said. 'How much am I getting?'

'Enough.'

'Give me a clue. Enough for me to go down for intent to supply?' I didn't wait for her to answer. 'On second thoughts, don't tell me,' I said. 'I'd rather not know.'

'Oh, Nick. I am sorry. I don't mean to get you into trouble.'

'Forget it. It's all part of the service. I'm sure I'll be OK.'

I hope I will, I thought.

'Are you going to take your car?'

'No way. It's too conspicuous. I'll get a cab. Pull one off the street.'

'Don't be paranoid, Nick.'

'If I wasn't paranoid, I'd be dead by now.'

'You know best.'

'You're right,' I said. 'I do.' I put the piece of paper with the address on it in my pocket, kissed her on the cheek and left. I went downstairs using the lift, and out through the front entrance past the reporters and photographers who didn't acknowledge my existence, and strolled out of the square looking for a cab. I didn't have far to look. I picked one up coming along Brompton Road, and told him to drop me off at the corner of Smith Street and the King's Road. It was a pleasant day. Pleasant enough to make me think that if I got my collar felt with a load of smack, how much I'd miss my freedom.

After I'd paid off the cab, I wandered down Smith Street just like a tourist. The address I was looking for turned out to be a pleasant, small, white-painted terraced house. I didn't waste time going past and back again. But I went slowly enough to check out the parked cars on both sides of the road, and didn't spot any suspicious-looking geezers in unmarked Ford Sierras. Mind you, if the place was under surveillance, Old Bill had had a lot more time to set it up than I had to suss it out.

I climbed the stone steps to the front door and rang the bell. As I waited I clocked the houses opposite. That's where they'd be, if they were anywhere. Ninotchka had been right, I was paranoid.

The door opened behind me and I spun on one heel. I found myself looking at a fat, ginger-headed party with long sidies, half a dozen chins, the bottom one of which almost covered a puce bow tie at the neck of a blue-and-white-striped shirt that would have made a duvet cover for a kingsize bed. His gut was amazing. He blocked the entrance to the hall like a sumo wrestler 'Elmo'? I queried.

'Who wants him?' His voice was surprisingly high, coming from such a massive frame.

'Nick.'

'Come in, do. He's expecting you.' He did a three-point turn in the narrow passage and led the way back through the house. I closed the front door behind me.

We did a sharp right into a tiny room stuffed full of furniture covered with bric-à-brac. One sideboard in particular, standing opposite the door, groaned with china ornaments, little animals made out of spun glass, photographs in tiny silver frames, wax fruit, and all sorts of other crap.

Sitting on a pile of Moroccan cushions in one corner, in front of a TV and video hook-up, sat a precious-looking youth in leather trousers and a white silk shirt. His highlighted hair hung around his shoulders and down to the middle of his back. He was rolling a joint on a lacquered tray balanced in his lap, and watching *Neighbours*. 'A visitor for you, Elmo,' carolled the fat man. 'A nice man named Nick.'

Elmo squinted at me through his fringe. 'For Nin, yeah?' he said.

I nodded.

'Can I get you a coffee, Nick, and perhaps a sugared biscuit?' asked the fat man.

'No, thanks. I ate at the office.'

'Gloria,' said Elmo, 'get lost for fuck's sake. I've got business and you make me nervous.'

'Charmed,' said Gloria, turned, and followed his belly out of the room.

'Wanker,' said Elmo. And for a moment I didn't know if he meant me or Gloria.

He finished rolling the joint and stuck it into his mouth and lit it using a disposable lighter. 'Big trouble back at the ranch?' he said.

I nodded.

'Too fucking weird. Guy gets a stake through his heart. It was on the news.'

'Strange but true.'

'Like a late-night horror movie on TV.'

'Yeah,' I agreed again.

'Puts a strain on my business.'

'I'm sure Turdo would sympathise if he was still alive.'

'Yeah. Bad vibrations. Still, he was only a roadie. They're just like number eleven buses. Always another along in a minute.'

'It's a point of view.'

'Want some of this?' He offered me the joint.

'No thanks,' I replied. I think it would have choked me.

'Sure,' he said. 'Business before pleasure, right?'

'Right.' I just kept on agreeing. It was one of the most agreeable conversations I could ever remember having. 'You've done a lot of business at Jones' since the band arrived?' I asked.

'Sure. Mega.'

'Were you there on Monday night?'

He wrinkled his brow as he considered the question. 'Could've been,' he said after a minute. 'I'm there a lot.'

'I can imagine. But Monday?'

'Almost certainly.'

'Doing deals?'

'Yup.'

'With whom?'

Just as he was about to answer Gloria came back in with a pinny the size of Surrey spread over his massive belly. He was wearing pink rubber gloves and holding a plastic washing-up brush in one hand. 'Are you sure there's nothing I can get you, Nick?'

'Piss off, you fucking fat old queen,' said Elmo viciously. 'Go and polish your wok or something.'

Petulant. I know the type. I was married to one for long enough.

Gloria pouted. 'Elmo dear,' he said, 'don't be so nasty. Your friend Nick will think less of you if you are.'

'So fucking what?'

'Well, if you're going to be like that, I'll get back to the dishes.' And he left.

'You make a nice little living at all this.'

'I get by.'

'You supply a lot to *Pandora's Box*?'

'Amongst others.'

'Like who?'

'Visiting bands, diplomats, the royal family… you know the scene. You don't get a house like this at my age,' he gestured around the room, 'punting spangles to kids outside school gates.'

'This is your place?'

'Sure.'

'I would have thought…'

'Then you thought wrong,' he interrupted. '*I* own the real estate. Gloria does the cooking and cleaning and pops down the shops. He's very big on popping down the shops. He's very big on everything as a matter of fact. He's OK. He earns his keep.'

'I'm glad to hear it,' I said. 'And talking of earning your keep, where's the gear I'm supposed to collect?'

Elmo scrabbled around amongst the cushions and came up with a brown envelope. He tossed it to me, and I caught it one handed. I opened the flap. Inside were half a dozen wraps. I took one out and opened it. It looked like brown sugar.

'OK?' he asked.

'Seems to be. I'm no connoisseur.'

'Nin is.'

'And who else is that I might know?'

'Why are you so nosey?' he asked. A reasonable question under the circumstances, I thought.

'Habit.'

He tensed. Wrong, Nick, I thought.

'Relax,' I said, 'I'm not a copper. Just tell me who you've been selling to.'

'That's privileged information.'

'So's this address. But I've got it, and I can pass it on to any one of several interested parties I can think of.'

'Go ahead. Then I'll drop Ninotchka right in it. Don't think I wouldn't.'

I believed he'd sell his gran'ma for a kilo of sinsemilla. But I also believed, just from the look of him, that he'd tell me everything he knew if he was threatened with violence.

'Elmo,' I said, 'if you don't tell me who you supplied dope to in that hotel I'm going to pick you up and put your head through that window without opening it first. It'll spoil your pretty face, believe me.' I was tempted to do it anyway. Perhaps I would, just for badness. Just for what he'd said about Turdo.

He looked at me, all toughed up and spaced out as fuck. This time he took my word for it. Smart guy.

So he told me.

'Thanks,' I said, when he'd finished, and turned to go. Gloria was standing behind me, filling the doorway. Still in his pinny and rubber gloves, but he'd dumped the washing-up brush and found a wicked-looking kitchen knife with a blade about ten inches long that twinkled in the light.

I stood still. Just raised my hands in a deprecating way. Out of the corner of my eye I saw Elmo smile.

'You slag,' said Gloria. 'Threatening my baby.'

'Your baby sucks shit, Gloria,' I said. 'Sucks shit and fucks shit. You fat, ugly old cunt.'

'Bastard!' he spat, and came at me, knife hand foremost. I moved to one side, caught his wrist and let his bulk carry him past me. I didn't let go, and the bone snapped like a celery stick. He screamed and ran full tilt into the knick-knack-covered sideboard. All his little treasures that were on it went flying. His other little treasure started to come to his feet, and I did exactly what I'd wanted to do to Pandora. I drop kicked him between the eyes and he flew backwards over the pile of cushions and landed on top of the TV and video. The whole lot went over in a shower of sparks.

I picked up the knife, stuck it between the door and jamb, snapped off the blade and dropped the handle on the floor. 'Bye now,' I said to Elmo. 'You'd better get Gloria an ambulance. If he doesn't get that wrist in plaster he won't be able to rinse out your smalls properly.' And I left.

I walked up the King's Road and into The Chelsea Potter. I bought a beer and drank half of it. Then I went into the gents and into a stall and transferred a small amount of the heroin from one of the wraps into an envelope I found in the pocket of my jacket.

Then I went looking for another cab.

20

I got the cabbie to take me to the Cromwell, and wait. Once inside I asked for the doctor who'd looked after Shapiro during his stay. I was in luck. He was on duty. I found him in his office. I gave him the envelope and asked him to compare the sample inside with the heroin that had been found in Shapiro's suite, that he'd had analysed. He agreed to do it. I went back to the cab and on to Jones'.

I delivered the gear to Ninotchka, then felt so lousy about just about everything that I went back to my suite, stuck a 'Do Not Disturb' sign on the door handle, yanked the phone and closed all the curtains. Then I went to bed. And that was that until I woke up with a freezing cold flannel in my face. I was dreaming about drowning, and when I came to, I was. You know how that is? When you're suddenly woken up. I came awake like I'd been trapped under fifteen fathoms of black water. I was literally swimming on dry land. Pumping my arms and legs. I heard a yelp and saw Ninotchka jump backwards away from the bed. 'What the hell...?' I said.

'You nearly punched me out, you big goon,' she yelled.

I found myself sitting up in bed, tangled up in the sheet, naked except for my shorts, with a wash cloth around my neck, dripping ice-cold water down my chest. I was soggy, sleepy and as confused as shit. 'What *is* happening?' I demanded.

'Slow down,' said Ninotchka, and started to laugh. You've heard about holding your sides. She did. It was about two minutes later, and I'd straightened the bed clothes, and dried myself with a corner of the sheet, and thrown the flannel on to the bedside table, before she recovered. 'Shit,' she gasped. 'Oh, Nick, that was the best.'

'What are you doing here?' I said.

'You're taking me to dinner, remember? No one could get an answer out of you. I got the pass key from the manager. You were sleeping like a baby. You looked so sweet...'

'You could hardly bear to wake me, I know.'

'I wasn't going to be stood up.'

'What time is it?'

'Almost nine.'

'What time's dinner?'

'Nine o'clock.'

'We're going to be late then. Let's not bother.'

'The later the better. I hate being on time.'

'Just as well, because we won't be. I need a shower. If you'll wait in the other room...'

'Are you shy?'

'Yes. Now get out of here, will you?'

She went.

I got out of bed and went to the bathroom. I looked in the mirror and blanched. Still, nothing that a little Vaseline on the lens wouldn't cure.

After a shave, shower and shampoo I looked and felt a little better. I put on my robe and went to choose an outfit. I wanted to wear the tie that Ninotchka had bought me, so I picked a plain midnight blue single-breasted suit, a white shirt with a tab collar, black socks and black loafers. I knotted the tie and stepped back to admire my reflection in the mirror. Not bad, even if I did say so myself. When I'd checked the visuals, I went into the sitting room. 'Who are you, and where's Nick?' asked Ninotchka, who was sitting on the sofa cuddling what looked like a gin and tonic.

'Humorous,' I said. 'You Americans aren't usually known for your cutting wit.'

'How about Steve Martin?'

'Give me a break.'

'Robin Williams?'

'Maybe.'

'Pee Wee Herman?'

'Let's go to dinner,' I said, and offered her my arm. When she stood up, she said, 'Do you like my dress?' and did a quick twirl. It was black, made of satin and lace, with a short, full skirt over loads of petticoats, and a tight bodice that pushed her breasts up and out. With it she wore black tights and elastic-sided ankle boots.

'You look like Annie Oakley on a night out,' I said. 'A regular cowgirl.'

'That's just what I wanted you to say. Let's go knock 'em dead.' And she took my arm and we left the room.

The meal was a little strange to say the least. Ninotchka and I were the last to arrive. When we got downstairs, the hotel manager was waiting for us. He showed us not to the regular restaurant but to a large annexe at the side of it. One huge round table dominated the room. It had been set for twenty-two, and twenty people were sitting round it. They all gave us a good clock as we waltzed in.

The middle of the table was dominated by a coloured ice sculpture in the shape of two life-sized guitars crossed like swords. 'Wow!' said Ninotchka, pinching my arm painfully. 'That's amazing. A Vox Teardrop, and a Gretsch Double Anniversary. They look so real.'

'Awesome,' I said.

As we walked to the table, Pandora stood up. 'Ninotchka,' he said, 'we thought you weren't coming. Wonderful dress. And Nick too. You must tell me where you got that tie.'

He was wearing a red tartan suit, black shirt and a matching tartan tie. He looked horrible. 'Come and sit down,' he went on, and a waiter ran forward to pull back our chairs.

When we were comfortably seated I checked out the rest of the diners. Ninotchka was on my right. On my left was Box's wife, Barby. She was wearing a little black Lycra dress which showed most of the tops of her breasts. She smiled at me and said hello. And I smiled, and said hello back, and tried not to look at her cleavage for too long. Although it was tempting. Next to her was Box himself, then Lindy Hopp next to her husband. She wiggled her fingers in greeting. He gave me a wry smile. Next to Shapiro was a woman I didn't know, then a long-haired geezer I didn't know either, in a Lurex jacket and shades, who was chewing at his nails like the kitchen staff had just gone on strike. On his far side was a straight-looking matron dressed in something green that looked like it had gone off when she wasn't looking, sitting next to Louis Pascall, the American lawyer.

Then in a little enclave were Pandora, sitting between the two teenyboppers, with their mother next to them. All four ignored me. On their left was a glamorous-looking blonde who was fixing her lipstick. Then Lomax who flashed us a big smile. Then yet another woman I'd never seen. She looked like one of the three witches from *Macbeth* on dict pills. Sitting next to her was Tony Tune, the record producer I'd met the day before. He nodded to me. I nodded back. Then there was a fat guy in full evening dress with a wing collar, and what was obviously his date, a knockout redhead in a purple dress that made me want to get acquainted quick and check her zips. Finally there was a bloke with very long hair in a leather jacket, and next to him on Ninotchka's other side a stunning-looking brunette in a see-through white blouse with no bra. The pink tips of her nipples were plainly visible as she moved. Which she kept doing like she had ants in her pants. If she was wearing any. And that was it. It was like a crowd scene from *The Ten Commandments*. Cecil B DeMille where are you when we really need you?

'Christ, sort this lot out for me, will you?' I said to Ninotchka.

'Who don't you know?'

I pointed them out. She explained. The fingernail biter was Baby Boy Valin, the drummer. He was sitting next to his girlfriend. The witch lookalike was Scratch, the other female vocalist. The glamorous blonde was one of Lomax's string of girlfriends. The guy in evening dress was Spike Leonard, the president of Cobra Records, who released *Pandora's Box* worldwide. The redhead was one of the PRs from the record company. The rock and roller with all the hair was

Shorty Long, the bass player. Plus groupie. As Ninotchka gave me the rundown, a waiter hovered to take our order for drinks. I opted for a whisky sour. Ninotchka went for more gin.

As the waiter shot off to the bar, Pandora stood up. 'Welcome, people,' he said. 'I'm not going to make a speech, but just a few words now that everyone's here.' He looked over at Ninotchka and me as he spoke. 'This is not the happiest day in the history of the band. But we've come through worse. Much worse. After due consideration and consultation with Spike there,' the gent in evening clothes nodded his head, 'and Tony, and our advisors, and the members of the band and road crew – we've decided to stay on in London and finish the album.' He paused. If he'd expected applause, he was disappointed. 'And tonight we go out and tell the world that *Pandora's Box* is alive and well, and will outsell everyone else on the planet this autumn. We start with a visit to *The Miracle's* reception this evening. It's due to start at midnight, after they've finished their gig at Wembley Arena. I've ordered limos for that time. We'll make a grand entrance about twelve thirty. *Pandora's Box* en masse. We'll blow the fuckers away. *The Miracle* – what a pile of shit! They couldn't get arrested with their last album, and from what I hear they've papered the walls for tonight's show. The scalpers are *paying* people to take tickets off their hands. We, on the other hand, have sold out the same gig for five nights in a row. What more can I say? Class tells. Now enjoy your meal. I intend to.' He clapped his hands. The doors to the kitchen opened and a stream of waiters burst through, each carrying two trays above his head.

'Gipsy violins next,' said Ninotchka. 'Or fire eaters or some such.'

'I wouldn't be surprised at anything. The geezer's really full of himself tonight. I suppose that's because you're staying. The last I heard there was an exodus being planned back to LA.'

'Keith convinced me not to go. He can be very persuasive.'

Looking round the table and knowing that Pandora had been inside the knickers of at least four of the eleven women present, that I knew about, I couldn't help but agree.

The meal was OK. Pandora had obviously got that organised

too. For starters it was satay with peanut sauce, chillis, rice cake and slices of purple onion, or watercress soup. The main course was a choice between lamb cutlets in a mint and orange sauce, mange tout stuffed with crab meat, or a single baby chicken braised in Calvados. Each came with a choice of vegetables. For dessert there was lemon and lime sorbet or chocolate pudding rotten with rum. There was a selection of fine wines, coffee and liqueurs. I had the satay and the lamb.

As I was eating I noticed that Tony Box was really getting into the vino collapso. He'd finished two bottles before the main course arrived. As I was trying to find some meat on my nouvelle-cuisine chop, he leaned over to me, pushing Barby out of the way as he did so. 'What time are we on tonight?'

I stopped with my fork an inch from the plate. I looked at Barby, who made one of those faces that people do when a lunatic starts talking to himself on the tube. 'Sorry?' I said.

'What time?' he asked again.

'What? The reception?'

'No, the gig. You're the fucking tour manager! Don't we pay you enough to know a simple thing like that?'

'I'm not the tour manager,' I said.

'Then what the fuck are you doing here?'

'Trying to eat my dinner,' I said. I was beginning to get pissed off. All the other conversations at the table had stopped and everyone was looking towards us. Lomax came to the rescue. He got up from his seat and came around to where we were. 'Hey, big Box,' he said. 'What's up?'

'Wanker can't do his job.'

'Well, he's new, man. Give him time. What's the problem?'

'What time are we on?'

'Don't worry about a thing. There's hours yet. Leave it to me. I'll give a shout when we need you.'

'I've got to get changed,' said Box.

'Trust me.'

'OK,' nodded Box and stuck his snout back into his glass. Slowly the other conversations resumed.

Lomax slapped me on the shoulder and winked. 'OK, tour manager?'

'Safe,' I said.

'Good. That's what I like to hear.'

Barby leant over and whispered in my ear. 'Sorry about that. He gets a bit funny sometimes.'

I shrugged. 'No problem.'

I turned to Ninotchka. 'Is he always like that?' I asked. 'I thought he was pretty weird when I first met him, but he's totally spaced out tonight.'

'Some days are worse than others. Poor Tony. He shouldn't mix the juice with the dope.' She sighed. 'But he'll never change. He's been in detox so many times he's got a gold card. And I'm sure he only goes to AA to see his old buddies.'

'Bitchy,' I said.

'Not really. You should hear him when he starts on me and men. He's OK, the best one of the lot. We understand each other.'

'Only some days are better than others, by the looks of it.'

'That's right.'

I skipped dessert, and ordered coffee and Grand Marnier. I was chatting to Ninotchka about something or other when Pandora stood up. 'Right,' he said, 'I've got a surprise for you all.'

As he said it, the main doors to the annexe burst open and two women dressed in black basques, suspenders, black fishnet stockings and black high-heeled shoes burst in. Both carried silver trays upon which were piled parcels covered in silver paper and decorated with ornate silver bows. They made straight for the table. 'What's going on now?' I asked.

'God knows,' said Ninotchka. 'Another of Keith's little surprises, I expect.'

'Has this geezer got a degree in bad taste?' I asked.

The pair came up to the table and handed out a parcel to each of us. There was much tearing of paper and oohing and aahing going on. Even I got one. It was small but heavy. When I opened it I found a velvet box. Inside was a gold Rolex with a black face and diamonds for numerals. It felt like the real thing. Ninotchka had the ladies' version, as they so coyly put it. All around the table it was the same. The men had the larger model, the women the smaller. 'Christ!' I said. 'Are they real?'

'Keith wouldn't mess with fakes,' said Ninotchka. 'It would dent his ego.'

'These are about ten grand apiece,' I said. 'That's over two hundred thousand pounds.'

Ninotchka shrugged. 'He likes making extravagant gestures.'

'Shit, I should say he does.' I put on the watch. I must say it looked the business.

Pandora stood up again. 'A small token of my appreciation for your hard work and loyalty.' This time he got the applause he wanted. Funny what a load of gold jewellery will do. Everyone clapped except Tony Box. He hadn't bothered to open his gift, just tossed it on the table in the wreckage of his meal and half the wine cellar. Suddenly he came to his feet and stood weaving there, one hand on the table to support himself. The applause died out.

'Bollocks!' he shouted. 'Fucking bollocks, Keith.'

Barby put her hand on his arm, but he shook it off. 'Fucking loyalty,' he went on. 'You bastards don't know the meaning of the word. None of you.' And he leaned over and picked up the ice sculpture which was slowly melting away on the table, and holding it aloft moved away from the table and heaved it through the closed window of the annexe where it burst into a million tiny splinters on the hard top outside, amongst the shards of glass and wood from the window frame. Everyone was silent. Box turned and stood swaying slightly like a tree in a strong breeze. Then Pandora grinned and started clapping his hands. One by one the rest of the people at the table joined in except Ninotchka and me. I really rated her for that. The rest were just licking arse. I looked over at her and shook my head. She shook her head back. As the applause died down, the hotel manager came into the room. He didn't even bother looking at the damage, but I would have bet he was mentally assessing it and adding it to the bill. Instead he went up to Pandora and whispered in his ear.

'The cars are here. Let's go,' he said. 'And make one hell of an entrance.'

Seeing the guy that night I realised why they called him The Tsar, and how *Pandora's Box* had lasted as long as they had. Everyone stood up and started milling around. I took Ninotchka's arm and tucked it under mine. 'That Box *is* crazy,' I said. 'What was all that about?'

'Rock and roll, Nick. Just rock and roll,' she said. 'Now, come on, it's party time. And you're my beau.'

21

We went outside, and parked at the kerb were eight black Mercedes 600 limousines converted to right-hand drive. Each was almost twenty foot long, and altogether they stretched the length of the street like a river of shiny cellulose. By the back door of each car was a Premiere man in full evening dress. It was quite a sight. Ninotchka and I were in the third car, with Chas driving and my old friend Don riding shotgun. He even demeaned himself so far as to be almost civil to me as I got in the car after Ninotchka. As we settled down in the back, I said, 'This is like *Alice In Wonderland*.'

'Lie back and enjoy it, Nick,' she said. 'You could be eating hamburger next week.' Never a truer word had been spoken. I've learned it's foolish to look a gift horse in the mouth, especially if it's got gold teeth. So I did as I was told and enjoyed the short ride to The Inn On The Park.

Even at that late hour there were enough people about for us to cause a stir. Eight long black German cars with darkened windows, headlights and spotlights on full beam, riding in convoy, is not something you see in London every night of the week. We rumbled up to the hotel and the doormen didn't know what had hit them. The *paparazzi* were out in force and Pandora and his merry bunch of men and women posed for all they were worth.

We rendezvoused in the hotel foyer. It was still busy and we got our fair share of attention. The reception was being held in the main ballroom and we teamed up in pairs with outriders of security men and cut a swathe through the guests, onlookers, groupies and disappointed twenty-four-hour-party people who couldn't get to the free booze. As we went in through the huge doors, Pandora and the blonde teenybopper to the fore, the hotel security just stepped back and let us pass. It was excellent timing. Everyone inside just stopped and gaped.

Once inside we all stood in the doorway and bathed in the glory, reflected or otherwise.

After a few minutes, when the novelty was over, Ninotchka bumped me with her hip. 'I'm off to fix my make-up,' she said. It was perfect, but I said nothing. Instead I wandered around to see what was happening. The first face I recognised belonged to Seltza. He was standing to one side of the door, leaning against the wall looking cool. I walked over and joined him.

'Hi,' I said.

He turned and grinned. 'Hi, man. I saw you come in with the high rollers.'

'That's me,' I said.

'It was quite an entrance. And that's quite a dress that our lovely blonde singer is wearing.'

'Sure is. Are you on your own?'

'Temporarily. Most of the crew are here. Boss's orders. They're around somewhere. But right now I'm on the prowl.'

'Anyone take your fancy?'

'Only the booze. I'm not really in the mood for women after what happened last night.' He kicked at the carpet with the pointed toe of his boot. 'I'm going to get a bottle and get as drunk as a skunk. And howl.'

'Do skunks howl?' I asked.

'Shit, I don't know. I come from Los Angeles.' He pronounced it with a hard 'g'. Angle-lees.

Ninotchka came out of the cloakroom. 'You'd better get front and centre, Nick. Your commanding officer has arrived,' said Seltza.

'Knock it off, Seltz. She's all right, believe me.'

'I'll take your word for it. See you.' And he slid along the wall away from me.

Ninotchka came over and grabbed my arm. 'Are you OK, Nick?'

'Yeah, sure.'

'Was that Seltza?'

'Yeah.'

'He doesn't like me. Every man who wants to fuck me and can't doesn't like me. And most who have, too. Do you like me, Nick?'

'Sure.'

'You won't. You'll change.' She shrugged. 'Everyone else has.'

'But you don't change?' I asked.

She looked at me with her beautiful blue eyes. 'Only my underwear,' she said. And winked lasciviously.

'Maybe you just need a friend,' I said.

'A man *friend*? That would be a first. But maybe I do. And maybe you're the man. Whaddya say?'

'I say, let's get stupid. The booze is free, the night is young, you're beautiful, and we have a lot of sorrows to drown.'

'Amen to that,' said Ninotchka, and we headed towards the bar.

Now, I've been to some receptions in my time for various things, but this was one of the biggest bunfights I'd ever seen. The ballroom had been decked out like some acid-head's idea of a dance hall in the deep south of America. The wooden floor was covered in sawdust. The lights were low. There were loads of neon bar signs on the walls, and Stars and Stripes and Confederate flags all over the shop. The bar served only jugs of margaritas, champagne, Schlitz, Rolling Rock, Bud, Southern Comfort and Jack Daniel's, which suited me down to the ground. The food was southern too: fried chicken, ribs, crayfish, gumbo, poor boy sandwiches with oysters and piquant sauce, and great tubs of coleslaw and salad. All served by gents in long white aprons and tall white hats, assisted by waitresses in gingham dresses, stetsons and cowboy boots.

Ninotchka's outfit fitted in perfectly. In one corner of the room was a stage draped with more flags, and a cajun band were giving it plenty of zydeco and western swing tunes. By this time the party was beginning to roar, and the first casualties were already appearing.

Pandora had acquired a water pistol from somewhere which he kept loading with neat JD from the bar. Then he went round spraying it in people's drinks and even their open mouths if they were game. And lots were. One or two people were going to go through the pain barrier before the night was through.

'So what's this band *The Miracle* all about?' I asked Ninotchka, once we were comfortably the right side of a couple of glasses.

'Don't you know?'

'Sorry,' I apologised.

'Shit kickers, son,' she explained. 'Good old southern boys. That's what this is all in aid of.' She gestured round the room. 'Lots of hair and not much talent. They want to be *Guns 'n' Roses* or *The Stones*. No way. File under "Fell at the First Fence". They're over there. Check them out.' She pointed at four geezers in faded, torn, tight denim and an assortment of Oxfam rejects, standing close to the stage. One was wearing a red sequined tail coat. Another, a tiny little brat, was in a Confederate officer's jacket and had a shiny black top hat perched rakishly on top of his feather cut. They all had long locks. One in particular's tawny mane reached almost to his waist. Each had a blonde babe on his arm. 'They don't like us much,' said Ninotchka. 'We stole too much of their thunder when we came in.'

'Looks like they've got some dough to afford all this, though.'

'Flash. The record company panicking. You heard what Keith said. He may be a bastard, but he's a shrewd one. He knows the value and sales to the nearest ten cents of the top fifty bands in the world.'

'Where do *The Box* stand in that?'

She shrugged and looked at the ceiling. 'Top ten.'

'Not bad.'

'It keeps me in French perfume.'

'I thought I was doing that.'

'You're sweet. Can you smell it?'

'I'm drunk with the fragrance.'

'I thought it was the wine you had with dinner.'

As we stood there chewing the fat, people kept coming up to Ninotchka and trying to engage her in conversation. She blanked most of them out. I thought that to be that rude and get away with it was the benchmark of a true star. Eventually someone did get her attention, a brittle blonde from On Line Publicity. Her name was Dorothy and she looked like she'd been hung out to dry in the sun, so emaciated and wrinkled was she. 'Darling,' she said to Ninotchka, giving me an arch look, 'we must talk photo opportunities.' I swear she said that, and without a trace of a horse's laugh.

Ninotchka looked at me. 'Sorry, Nick,' she said. 'Duty calls.'

'When you gotta go, you gotta go,' I said. 'I'll catch you on the merry-go-round.' She kissed me on the cheek, and Dorothy led her away to a quiet corner.

As I was looking round the room, Pascall, the American lawyer, buttonholed me. 'Good evening,' he said. 'How's it going?'

'I think you know.'

'Not good?'

'The worst.'

'I hoped it wouldn't come to this.'

'Shit happens,' I said.

'So true.'

'But at least you still have a band.'

'If all goes well.'

'You think it won't?'

'As you rightly say, "shit happens".'

'I'm doing my best to see that it doesn't.'

'I know, Mr Sharman, and as I said before you have my backing one hundred per cent.'

'That's good to know.'

'If you require anything, my door is always open.'

'I'll remember that.'

'And now I see that my wife needs me.' I looked round. The woman in green who'd been sitting next to him at dinner was waving in our direction. 'Enjoy yourself, Mr Sharman,' he said.

'I will.'

He excused himself and left.

With no sign of Ninotchka returning I decided to go and look for adventure.

What, or rather who, I found instead was Chris Kennedy-Sloane.

He was an accountant and investment consultant who specialised in the music business. He was a bit of a reptile, but a likeable one. That night he was all dolled up in the latest line in crushed silk gent's suiting and baseball boots. He looked like he didn't know whether he was on his way to his office or the gym. 'Chris, my old friend,' I said, 'what the hell are you doing here?'

'Nick! Well, I'll be damned,' he said. 'I thought that was you making a dramatic entrance with *The Box,* but I didn't believe my eyes. How the devil are you?'

'Just fine. So tell me, I thought you hated dos like this?'

'Quite right. But I'm trawling about for some new money. Things are tough at the minute.'

'*The Miracle*?' I asked.

'I don't know,' he said. 'They're slipping fast in my opinion.'

'So I heard.'

'Did you? Interesting.'

'So?'

'Just casting a wide net. Business is business.'

'Caught anything?'

'Maybe. But it's a bit hush-hush at the moment. I can slip it to you later if you like. Big bucks.'

'I think I've had it slipped to me enough for one lifetime, Chris,' I said. 'But thanks for the offer.'

'Now, more to the point, what are *you* doing here? As if I didn't know. That business with the roadie and the drumstick, is it?'

'That's it.'

'Thought so. Nasty that. Makes me go quite cold just to think about it.'

'I saw it. How do you think I feel?'

'And you've been brought in on the case.'

I nodded.

'Fancy that. First Mark McBain, now *Pandora's Box.* My dear boy, you should open an office on the West Coast. I could arrange a sub-let for you, if you like.'

'Ha-ha,' I said. 'But listen, Chris, I'm glad I bumped into you. You're just the man.'

'My heart's sinking already. Just the man for what?'

'I want to know a little more about *The Box*.'

'Like what?'

'Anything. Idle gossip. Malicious rumour. Hard fact. The sort of things you deal in every day.'

'I'm flattered. But now you mention it, apparently there's plenty to know.'

'Is that right? Like what?'

'Money troubles. Internal feuding. Rumours of break-ups. Madness. Death. That sort of thing. An everyday story of pop music folk.'

'Can you find out more?'

'If I have to.'

'*Have* to.'

'What's in it for me?'

'Who knows?'

'Who indeed. All right, Nick, I'll find out what I can.'

'When?'

'Give me time. Today's Thursday. Well, Friday morning really. Call me Monday.'

'Monday may be too late.'

'You intrigue me. Tell me more.'

'I'll tell you when I see you. How about later today? This evening.'

'It must be urgent. All right, I'll see what I can do, as it's for an old friend. But you don't give me much time. Come to my office. You've never been there, have you?' He reached into his breast pocket and gave me a card. I glanced at it. The address was in Docklands. I could picture it already. 'Drop by about six. Drinks in the boardroom.'

'I'll be there,' I said. 'Look, I'd better get back to Ninotchka. I'm supposed to be keeping an eye on her tonight.'

'I could keep an eye on her anytime.'

'Very funny. Six o'clock this evening, right?'

'Right.'

'Very good,' I said and went to get another drink.

The Miracle were loitering with intent around the bar. They were still fully accessorised with a bottle and a babe each. The one with most hair grabbed me by the lapel with the hand that held the bottle. I could smell the fumes from either its mouth or his. Whichever, it wasn't pleasant. 'You with that chick, Ninotchka?' he asked.

'Yes,' I said, untangling myself from his grasp.

'Good screw.'

I wondered if his comment was a statement or a question. I shrugged and turned to catch the barman's eye over his shoulder.

The one with the top hat picked up the conversational banter without a fumble. 'Fucking A,' he said.

I knew that I didn't have to protect Ninotchka's reputation. It preceded her like a fanfare of trumpets. But I must confess I didn't like these guys. I looked at the geezer with the top hat, and his beaky little face with the black thatch sticking out from under the brim of it, and I wanted to re-model his chin. 'Do you have to be an arsehole to be in your band?' I asked mildly.

'No, but it sure helps,' said the one in the red tail coat and they all dissolved into raucous laughter.

What was the point? I pushed past them and up to the bar.

'Pussy man,' said one of them, but I ignored it. It wasn't worth the trouble. I ordered a beer and the bottle was covered in ice and the liquid freezing. I drank it straight from the neck. Pussy? Me?

A voice from beside my shoulder said, 'You handled that well.' I looked round. A woman in a slinky cocktail dress stood beside me. She had short, shiny black hair cut in a bob. 'Dignity and strength,' she said.

'Hardly. More like indignity and weakness.'

'You'd only have been thrown out. They've got minders everywhere. They like to start fights and let other people finish them.'

'They're not the only ones,' I said.

'They'll pick on someone else in a minute, you'll see.'

I looked at her more closely. I didn't object to the view one bit.

'Have I got a smudge on my nose?' she asked.

'No,' I said. 'It's a very attractive nose as noses go, and totally smudge free.'

'I thought I had by the way you were looking.'

'Sorry,' I said. But I wasn't. 'My name's Nick. Nick Sharman.'

'I'm Carol Daley. But everyone calls me Sweetheart.'

'I'm not surprised.'

'Thank you.'

'It's a pleasure.' Then the penny dropped. 'Do you work for On Line?'

'That's right. How do you know?'

'I was talking about you the other day. I'm working for *The Box*.'

'Are you? So am I.'

'I know. You were in Danny Shapiro's suite on Monday night.'

She pulled a face. 'I was. I heard what happened. And that poor roadie.'

'It's getting the band's name in the papers.'

'Sure. But I'm not going back to that hotel 'til they catch who's doing it.'

'That's what I'm meant to be doing.'

'Are you a policeman?'

'Private.'

'How thrilling.' Thinking about thrilling her perked me up no end. 'Did you see anything strange that night?' I asked.

'No stranger than usual. We all sat around and got stoned and listened to music. I always get stoned when *The Box* are in town. I don't mean to, but you know how it is.'

I agreed that I did.

'I got a cab home about eleven,' she went on. 'I had an early call the next morning. The next thing was I heard from Lindy that Trash nearly died.'

'No one was acting strangely?'

'*Everyone* was acting strangely. That's the whole point, isn't it?'

Once again I had to agree. And that was more or less that. Another dead end.

'Are you going to be around for long?' she asked.

'What, tonight?'

'No, generally.'

'Christ knows. I'm surprised I've lasted this long.'

Ninotchka appeared at my elbow. 'Nick, I see you're talking to the best-looking woman in the room.'

'I always do,' I said. 'That's why I'm with you.'

'Flatterer.'

'Not at all.'

'What do you say, Sweetheart?' she asked.

'I think Nick's right.'

'I'd like to believe you, dear, but you're paid to say nice things like that.'

Meanwhile a little spat was flaring up about ten yards away from where we were standing. The guys from *The Miracle* were giving Tony Box a lot of stick at the other end of the bar. He had decided not to be as dignified or as strong as me. He might have been wasted, but he wasn't scared of them. Or maybe that was why he wasn't scared of them. And he had been looking for a fight all evening.

I saw the one with the most hair grinning, and the rest of the band laughed, and Box gave him a whack on the side of the jaw that sent him flying in one direction, his Bourbon bottle in another, and the blonde on his arm in yet another. He ended up in an undignified heap at the edge of the dance floor.

Aye, aye, I thought, and moved in the direction of the fracas. I wasn't the only one. From all corners of the room came other interested parties.

It was *The Boxes,* plus their security men and road crew, versus *The Miracle,* plus their security men and road crew. It could easily have turned into a pitched battle, like one of those saloon-bar brawls in the movies that would have suited the ambience of the place perfectly.

As we all squared off Ninotchka saved the day. She flounced through the crowd and stood between Box and the fallen member of *The Miracle* with her hands on her hips. 'Ah declare,' she said, and her voice took on a slight southern lilt, 'you two boys should be ashamed. Fussin' and feudin' when we should all be havin' a good time.' She held her hand out to the geezer on the floor. He looked at it for a second, then took it and she pulled him up. 'Now shake hands and be friends,' she said. 'Tony...' For the first time she wasn't quite so confident. 'Tony,' she said again. He mumbled something and stuck out his hand. The guy from *The Miracle* shook it. 'Good,' said Ninotchka. 'Now have a drink and let's hear no more of this nonsense.' And she flounced back to me again and the place relaxed and everyone moved away.

'Excellent,' I said.

She smiled. 'I've *still* got it,' she said. And she had.

After that, people started to leave in ones and twos. But Ninotchka was determined to party the night away. By the time she'd had enough, it was well past three and everyone else I knew was long gone, apart from Don, who was sitting on the edge of the stage looking like he wished he'd taken up a decent profession when he left school. Finally even Ninotchka had to give in. 'Nick,' she said, 'I'm bushed. Let's get the hell out of here.'

'Your word is my command.'

It was still dark, but only just, when we left the hotel with Don. There was only one Mercedes left in the street outside, and Chas was standing leaning against it. When he saw us he stood up straight and opened the back door. 'Sorry, Chas,' said Ninotchka. 'We lost track of time. Are we the last?'

He nodded. 'No problem, miss. I wouldn't do this job if I didn't like staying up late.'

'You're an angel.'

We got in the back, and Don got in on the front passenger side, and Chas drove us slowly back to the hotel through almost empty streets.

22

The limo slid to a halt outside the entrance to the car park. The barrier was down, blocking our way in. Dawn had just been a faint pink glow over the rooftops as we'd turned under the arch into the mews and the lights mounted on metal poles were still lit, and made dark shadows on the cobbles. The gatekeeper's hut was deserted. Chas tapped the horn lightly. Definitely illegal at that time of night. I hoped the neighbours wouldn't complain. No one showed. He turned to Don and said something we couldn't hear. Don glanced into the back of the car. He looked worried. Ninotchka leaned forward and pressed the button that lowered the partition between us and the driver's compartment.

'Something wrong?'

'There should be one of our blokes here. I don't understand it. Lock your doors, I'm going to check.'

'Want me to come?' I asked.

'No. Stay here. Look after Miss Ninotchka. Will you wind up the partition, miss? I don't want to take any chances. If there's no one about, we'll drive round the front.'

'Maybe we'd better do that now?' I suggested.

'I'll just take a quick look,' said Don. 'I'll stay near to the car. Now please close all the windows and lock your doors.'

Ninotchka did as she was told, and closed the partition. I slipped the lock on my door, and leant over and did the same on her side. All of a sudden I wished I had a gun handy.

Don got out of the car. He unholstered his pistol and held it in his right hand. Chas kept the engine running. Don squeezed through the gap between the barrier and the fence and walked to the hut. He tried the door knob and the door opened. He looked down, then back to the car, and waved his gun hand, gesturing us away. I hit the button to lower the partition. Chas stuck his head out of the open driver's window, and as the partition slid down I heard Don shouting: 'Get back. Get away. Go! Go! Go!' Chas stuck the column-mounted gear shift into reverse and slammed his foot down on the accelerator. The limo stalled. He'd given it too much gas.

I saw Don move his head, and look behind the car down the mews, and lift his gun. I looked through the back window as Chas ground at the starter. Someone was running towards the car. A shadowy, frightening figure with wild hair and limbs that looked too long for his body. As he ran his shadow lengthened across the ground which seemed to make him look even more frightening. He slammed against the back of the car and spreadeagled across the boot, and his face pressed close up to the tinted glass. The angle of the floods around the car park lit up his face. He looked crazed. Eyes wide and staring. A straggly beard. Filthy, matted hair and a gap-toothed mouth open in a silent scream. Ninotchka's wasn't. She looked back and put her hands to her mouth and cried an awful cry. As she screamed the starter caught and Chas put the car into gear and we sped backwards, picking up the figure as we went.

Chas was looking back through the open partition, his eyes as wide as those of whoever was leeched to the back of the car. The huge car veered crazily from side to side, and the bumper caught one of the tubs outside a mews house door. It exploded, and dirt showered the back of the vehicle. 'Stop!' I shouted, and he hit the brakes and the figure was catapulted off the boot.

He rolled and came to his feet, and ran off away from us. I heard the clatter of footsteps and Don ran past the car in pursuit. I slipped the lock on my door, opened it and got out. I ran towards the car park, jumped over the barrier and went to the hut. The door was jammed open by the body of a Premiere security man. I didn't recognise him. His throat had been torn out. The floor of the hut was slick with blood. I didn't bother looking for vital signs. He was dead.

I turned and ran back to the car. Chas sat in the front looking shocked. I slammed my hand on the door sill. 'Round the front,' I shouted. 'Quick!' He didn't respond. I opened the door and pushed him across the bench seat and got in behind the wheel. I reversed the car fast down the mews, then out under the arch, and it screamed up the wrong side of the street, and skidded to a halt outside the main door. I didn't bother with Chas. I jumped out of the car, opened the kerbside back door and dragged Ninotchka out, up the steps, through the doors and into the foyer. Two more Premiere men were in the lobby. I quickly told them what had happened, brushing aside their questions. One got on the radio, the other hit the phone on the reception desk. I bundled Ninotchka into the lift and up to her suite.

When we were inside she came into my arms and burst into tears. I held her close. She was sobbing and shaking so hard it was difficult to make out what she was trying to say. Eventually she calmed down a little. 'Nick,' she said. 'Nick… My God, I knew him.'

'Who?'

'That guy. That guy out there.'

'You knew him?'

'Yes.'

'Are you sure?'

'Of course I'm sure!'

'Who was he?'

'Bobby. Bobby Boyle.'

'Who?'

'Our old drummer.' And I remembered what the roadies had talked about at dinner. When was it, one, two days ago? Everything was starting to merge together like a bad dream.

'Christ,' I said, and she started to cry again.

23

I sat Ninotchka down, and went to the bar and poured a couple of drinks. Two very large brandies. After what we'd been through I thought we deserved them. And even if we didn't, I for one needed something, and by the look of it so did she. The adrenalin rush seemed to have negated the night's alcohol intake. I felt stone-cold sober. And stone cold. The glass rattled against Ninotchka's teeth as she took a sip. When the colour started to return to her face, I said, 'Are you absolutely sure you recognised that guy?'

She nodded.

'I can't believe it. He looked like a skipper to me.'

'A what?'

'A tramp. A derelict. One of the street people. The lucky few who sleep in the West End for free.'

'I'd recognise Bobby anywhere.'

'He didn't look like my idea of a rock star.'

'He's changed, Nick. He's been sick. He didn't used to look like that. He was pretty. Real pretty. He just took too much acid, that's all.'

'But even so.'

'Nick, I lived with the guy for six months. Some things you don't forget.'

'Are there any of these guys you haven't had an affair with?'

'Oh, Nick. For fuck's sake, don't be so straight.' She was the second person to call me that in a couple of days. Maybe I should grow a beard. 'That's the way it is,' she went on.

Outside I could hear the scream of sirens getting closer. 'In the wunnerful, fun world of rock and roll?' I said. 'It hasn't been much fun for some poor fuckers lately. You didn't see the state of the geezer in the car park.'

'God!' she said. 'That poor guy. I forgot.'

'It looks like your pal's number one suspect. Whatever you say.'

'No. Not Bobby.'

'Come on, Ninotchka. Give me a break.'

'No!'

'It's been a long time since you knew him.'

'No.'

'And you said yourself he'd taken too many drugs.'

'No,' she said again. 'Not Bobby. He's the gentlest guy I ever met.'

'People change.'

'Not that much. He couldn't do anything like that.'

The sirens were right outside now, whooping and hollering in the street below us.

'I have to tell the police,' I said.

'No. No, you can't!'

'Ninotchka, two people are dead.'

'Then I'll deny it. Say I was mistaken. It wasn't Bobby. It was what you said. A bum. Street trash.'

'Hell, Ninotchka, don't give me that crap. I'll still tell them what you said.'

'Don't.'

'And do what instead?'

'Try and find him yourself. He's hurting, Nick. Didn't you see his eyes?'

Yes, I thought. Mad eyes. Killers' eyes maybe. 'And if he kills again?'

'I keep telling you, he didn't kill anyone. Find him quickly and you'll know for yourself. Don't let the police get him first. They'll drive him even crazier. You can do it. You're good.'

162

'I'll think about it,' I said. 'I'll have to tell Roger.'

'Why?'

'Because he might have some idea where to start looking. He is the top man. Or at least the closest to the top that I trust.'

She smiled. She was beautiful when she smiled. Even through tear stains. 'You trust Roger?' she asked.

'Yeah.'

'I like you, Nick. D'you know that? You're a good judge of character.'

'I hope so.'

'Promise me then? Promise you won't tell.'

'OK,' I said reluctantly. 'But I'm definitely telling Roger what I'm up to.'

I used the phone. Lomax answered after the ninth or tenth ring. ''lo,' he said.

'Roger? Sharman.'

'What? What the fuck? Do you know what time it is?'

'What does it matter? The cops'll be waking you up soon enough. Can't you hear them?'

'Why? What the hell's happened *now?*'

I told him, as concisely as I could, leaving out any mention of Bobby Boyle. 'But I want to see you before they do,' I said when I'd finished.

'What about?'

'Not on the phone. Come up to Ninotchka's suite. I can't leave her alone, and Don is otherwise engaged.'

'I'll be right up.'

'Don't answer the phone again. Just get here.'

He arrived in less than five minutes. His thick hair was mussed and he had a dark five o'clock shadow. He was wearing jeans, a rugby shirt and a pair of Timberland shoes. 'What's up?' he asked as soon as I let him in. 'I should be downstairs. It sounds like all hell's breaking loose down there?'

'Drink?' I asked before answering.

'Perrier.'

I poured some into a tall glass over ice. 'Bobby Boyle,' I said as I handed it to him.

'What about him?'

'Where is he?'

'Slough, I think. I have an address for him. He lives with his father. Why?'

'Get it for me.'

'Why?' he asked again.

Then I told him the bits I'd left out on the phone. As I talked he kept looking from me to Ninotchka and back.

'Shit,' he said when I'd finished. 'Everyone thought he was all right.'

'How do you mean?' I asked.

'He was in a mental hospital. Paranoid schizophrenia was the diagnosis. But they seemed to have it under control. When Keith and I came over last year we visited him. He seemed fine. He was released a few months ago.'

'Christ!' I said. 'See, Ninotchka? The guy's as crazy as a coot.'

'No,' she said. 'He's not. He's just sick. I told you that.'

'Tell it to the men in white coats.'

'I don't care what you say, he still didn't kill anyone. Roger, you know him.'

Lomax shrugged. 'Years ago, sure. But now? Who the hell knows?'

'Nick's going to find him,' said Ninotchka, 'and prove he didn't have anything to do with any killings.'

'Yeah?' said Roger. 'But if he is going around murdering people...' He didn't finish the sentence.

'Yeah, I know, Rog,' I said. 'But I promised Ninotchka. Give me just a few hours. You say he's in Slough?'

'That's where we send his royalty cheques. He still gets plenty. His share of the big 'un. Ninotchka, we *should* tell the cops.'

'No,' she insisted.

'Listen,' I said, 'I've agreed to keep shtuum 'til I get a chance to check on this Bobby Boyle character. Let's leave it at that for now. OK?'

I saw Lomax open his mouth to argue, when we were interrupted by an urgent banging on the door.

24

Of course it was the cops, a pair of uniforms looking for the people in the car who had left the scene of the crime. When they saw Ninotchka, they removed their hats and began acting like a pair of groupies at a *Bay City Rollers* reunion. Ninotchka was the very soul of charm. I wouldn't have believed that she'd been scared half to death not thirty minutes earlier.

The coppers were not quite so polite to Lomax and me. But Lomax wasn't having any. He went straight to the phone and called up the top man in *The Dox*'s pet law firm. Not the Junior this time, you note, but the big cheese himself. When he got through, he handed the receiver to the nearest copper, who turned red, white, and then green in the space of half a minute. When the policeman had made doubly sure that the call was over, he replaced the handset as if it was made of spun sugar, smiled feebly at Lomax and asked us very politely if we'd mind terribly staying where we were until one of his superiors arrived.

We all agreed that we would stay. The policeman who'd taken the call then informed us that his colleague would be outside if we needed anything and both coppers left. 'Very good,' I said. 'I wonder what was said.'

Lomax gave me a look.

'To frighten him like that,' I continued.

'He didn't have to say much,' Lomax said. 'He's lunching with the Commissioner of the Met today, and dining with the Prime Minister tomorrow. And he didn't appreciate being woken up.'

'Our Prime Minister?' I asked.

'No, the Prime Minister of Lithuania. Of course your Prime Minister,' said Lomax sarcastically.

I was going to tell him that I was the one that did the witty lines, but I didn't. 'Well, he certainly put him in his place,' I said.

Ten minutes later Carpenter and Ripley arrived. They weren't so easily put off as the uniform, but were still wary, I could tell. I would have been too, in their shoes.

Ninotchka and I went through the whole story. Neither one of us mentioned Bobby Boyle. I still wasn't sure it was a good idea, but it was one of those times when, once you've started lying, you've just got to carry on, no matter how bitter the end might turn out to be.

Eventually we were allowed to go to bed. I suppose by that time it was just after six. I didn't. I just had a shower and some of Wilfred's coffee, and got ready to go to Slough. I found Lomax in his room, and he gave me the address I needed. He wasn't happy about it, but I got him to promise to keep quiet until I reported back with whatever I found, if anything. I suppose the last thing he needed right then was more scandal involving the band.

Then I went to the parking garage and got my car. It started first time, and I pulled it up the ramp and through the barrier into the mews. The gatekeeper's hut had been taped off and two policemen I hadn't seen before were keeping a pair of eyes on things. A couple of Premiere men were on duty just inside the fence. By then, I think anyone with any sense was working in twos. I was alone again as usual.

But then, sense was never my long suit.

25

S lough is a real shit hole, believe me. I think I read somewhere that once there was a plan to twin it with a public toilet in Belgrade, but the citizens of Belgrade turned down the deal. Slough is the sort of place that pit bull terriers go to die, but hardly, I thought, where ex-rock stars go to live. The address I was looking for was on the edge of the town. It was a three-up, three-down, red-brick dump in a street similar to every other street for miles. The front garden was three foot deep from wall to front window, and I pushed open the distressed wooden gate and knocked on the front door that last saw paint before litres took over from gallons and new pence from L.S.D.

There was no answer, so I knocked again. And somewhere, way back in the house, I heard a noise and saw some movement through the dusty pane of translucent glass.

I knocked for a third time and a tired old voice said: 'Who's there?'
I didn't answer the question. 'Mister Boyle?' I asked.
'That's right.'
'I want to talk to you about your son.'
'He's not here.'
My heart sank. 'Do you know where he is?'
'No.'
'Will you open the door?'
'Who are you?'

'My name's Sharman, I'm a private detective, and I'd like to talk privately.'

There was silence for a minute, but it seemed longer, and then the voice said again: 'Have you any identification?'

I took out one of my cards and put it through the letter box. Another minute, and I heard a rattling of chains and turning of locks, and the door cracked open. A face the colour of cigarette smoke, topped with greying hair, appeared in the gap.

'What about my son?'

'Can we talk inside?' I asked.

For a moment I thought he was going to slam the door in my face, and I wouldn't have blamed him if he had. But he sighed and pulled the door all the way open, and walked down the dingy hall away from me. I stepped inside, and closed it quietly behind me, and followed him into the first room on the right. It was small and untidy inside, with a grime of dust on every surface. The man stood on the faded carpet and faced me, and he seemed to have a grime of dust on every surface too. The room was hot, and smelled of old chip fat, and the curtains were drawn against the world. The television was on with the sound turned down low. A table lamp with a canvas shade decorated with a picture of Beachy Head was sitting on top of the TV, and its dim light illuminated a man who looked as if he'd just about had enough of the pain the world could give him. He was wearing a ratty cardigan with stains of food or snot down the front, over a yellowed shirt that had once been white, and dark blue trousers, greasy and wrinkled. His bare feet were stuffed into grey corduroy slippers. It was one of the most depressing sights I've ever seen.

'My son,' he said. 'What about him? Is he all right?'

'As far as I know, yes. But you say he doesn't live here?'

'I didn't say that. I just said he's not here now.'

'But he does still live here?'

'Yes.'

'How long since you last saw him?'

'A few days.'

'Do you remember exactly? It's very important.'

'No. Monday, Tuesday. Who knows?'

I pressed him. 'Please try and remember.'

'I tell you, I can't.'

He was agitated, so I changed tack.

'Does he often vanish for days at a time?'

He shrugged. 'Months sometimes. Years even. He was in a pop group. One day he lived with us, the next he didn't.'

At least I knew we were talking about the same bloke. 'Us?' I queried.

'Me and his mother. She died. A long time ago. He was never the same. He loved his mother.' The man sat down in an old armchair that faced the TV set. 'Why all these questions?' he said, more to the screen than to me.

'Two men have been killed this week. Someone says they saw your son at the scene of one of the murders,' I replied.

He looked away from the TV, and at me. 'Murder? You think my son had something to do with killing another human being?'

'I don't know. Do you?'

He didn't answer. 'Who were they?' he asked instead.

'One was a road manager with his old band *Pandora's Box*. The other was a security man at the hotel where they're staying in London. And on Monday it appears that someone tried to kill one of the guitarists with the band. They didn't succeed.'

'Those bastards,' he spat. 'They deserve everything they get.'

'Why?' I asked.

'They treated Bobby like dirt.'

'How?'

'They drove him crazy. Especially that damned Pandora. It was the drugs that did it. Then they dumped him.'

'They still pay him, I understand.'

'Money,' he said contemptuously. 'He thought they were his friends.'

That's life, I thought.

'But I heard he was being paid very well,' I said.

'So?'

'This house – it's not what I expected.'

'I know. You thought he'd live in a mansion.'

'Something like that.'

'He doesn't keep the money. He doesn't want anything from them.'

'What does he do with it?'

'He gives it away.'

'All of it?'

'Every penny.'

'Who to?'

He shrugged. 'Charities. The church. Sometimes he just walks around town handing out fifty-pound notes. That's why they put him away. They don't understand.'

'How do you live?'

'I have savings, and a small pension. We used to live in a bigger house. Bobby bought it for us years ago. I sold it and we moved here.'

'You don't try and stop him? Giving the money away, that is.'

'It's his money.'

Fair enough, I thought.

'You say someone saw him. Who?' asked Boyle.

'Ninotchka.'

For the first time I saw a ghost of a smile. 'She was the only decent one out of the lot of them. I thought they might get married, her and Bobby. He brought her to the old house a few times when they were in the country.'

'She still cares for him,' I said. 'She wouldn't tell the police she saw him. Or let me.'

'A good girl,' he said.

'But that doesn't change the fact that she recognised him. And a man had been killed just a couple of minutes before.'

'He wouldn't.'

'That's what she said.'

'You don't believe it?'

'I don't know, Mr Boyle. That's why I'm here. You say the band treated him badly. Do you think he's looking for revenge?'

The old man put his head in his hands and I heard him sob. His thin back shook.

'Mr Boyle?' I said.

He looked up at me and I saw tear stains like snail tracks on his cheeks. 'I don't know.'

'You say he was put away?'

'Yes.'

'In hospital?'

He nodded.

'A mental hospital?'

'Yes.' He looked ashamed. He needn't have been. I met some OK people when I was in one. But that was a long time ago. A different life. A different me.

'They said he'd be fine,' Boyle went on.

They always say that when they let you out, I thought. Sometimes they're right, and sometimes they're not.

'Can I see his room?' I asked.

'Why?'

'Why not?'

'I suppose so.' He stood up and led me upstairs. At the top was a door. He opened it. Inside, the curtains were drawn tight and the room was in darkness. Bobby Boyle's father reached in and switched on the overhead electric light. It was a big room. Two smaller ones knocked into one, I guessed. It smelt bad. A mixture of dirty bedding, dirty clothes and dirty human being. With one exception it was a tip. The bed was a tangle of grey sheets and stained blankets. There were clothes, papers, full ashtrays, empty beer bottles and cups rimed with dry tea or coffee, dustballs, and all sorts of other sleazy shit all over the place.

The exception filled one half of the room. It was a drum kit. But just to call it that was to belittle it. It was like calling a Rolls-Royce merely a car. It was quite literally the king of drum kits. The biggest I've ever seen by a mile. The drums were sprayed red, a bright, vulgar red with tiny specks of silver glitter in the finish that sparkled in the electric light. I went for a closer look. There were twin bass drums with a pair of tiny tom toms and two cow bells mounted on top. Behind them was a chrome snare, and a drum stool, and no less than ten variously sized floor-mounted toms, five on each side of the kit. There was a hi-hat, and fifteen ride, crash and zizzle cymbals spread around it at various heights. Every part of the kit was immaculate, made even more so by the squalor of the rest of the room. The drums were polished, the skins pure white, and the cymbals and stands gleamed in shades of gold and silver.

'He never plays it now,' said Boyle. 'Just polishes it. All day long when he's here. He just polishes it.' It was one of the saddest things I'd ever heard.

I walked round and stood behind the kit. It was like being in Fort Drums.

Attached to the two big tom toms at the back of the kit, hooked over the silver rims that held the skins tight, were leather holders for drumsticks. They were like long narrow knife sheaths, graded in size from small to large. There must have been twenty sets at least. The largest holders were empty.

'What happened to the sticks that go in these?' I asked.

'How do I know?'

'Do you know what size they were?'

He looked confused. 'Size? No, I don't. I don't know anything about drums.'

'Were they 2Bs?' I pressed.

'I tell you I don't know.'

Or care, I thought, and who could blame him? He'd lost a son. What were drumstick sizes compared to that? 'All right, Mr Boyle,' I said. 'It's OK, it doesn't matter.' But it did.

'Is that all?' he asked.

'For now. But I have to tell you, Mr Boyle, that I think the police will want to talk to your son.'

He didn't answer.

'So if you hear from him,' I went on, 'I suggest you tell him to contact them. It'll be better for him in the long run.'

He nodded, and stepped back out of the room.

All of a sudden I wondered if in fact Bobby Boyle was in the house. Then I mentally shrugged. There was nothing I could do about it if he was.

I followed Boyle downstairs, and he opened the front door for me. As I went out he said, 'Mr Sharman?'

I turned and stood on the doorstep. 'Yes?'

'If they find him and you're there, will you try and make sure they don't hurt him?'

That was when I knew he'd been telling the truth. He didn't know where his son was.

'Of course,' I said. 'Of course I will.' And I went back to the car.

26

I drove straight back to Jones'. By the time I got there it was almost midday. I passed through the police and security lines into the garage with no trouble. All was serene. At least there'd been no fresh bodies found, which was a relief to all. I parked up and went to my suite. I called the Cromwell, and got through to the doctor with whom I'd left the sample of smack the previous day. He confirmed that as far as the lab could ascertain, it came from the same batch as the heroin that Shapiro had OD'd on. Then I went looking for Ninotchka.

She was in her suite. Once again I got in with no trouble. I felt like I was golden. At least I did until we got into her office, and she turned on me. 'What the hell did you do to Elmo yesterday?' she demanded.

I had to think for a moment. 'What?' I said stupidly. I'd survived for so long without sleep I was having difficulty remembering who I was, let alone anything else.

'You broke his nose. And Gloria's wrist,' she said. 'They were at the hospital all day.'

It all came back to me. 'I hope it hurt,' I said. 'That fat freak tried to stick me with a carving knife.'

'You probably deserved it.'

'Charming! I was doing you a favour, remember? And by the way, you should get a new connection. He's selling you street shit. You should be careful of dealing with faggots. They're often unstable.'

'You are a bastard,' she spat.

'At times. Who isn't? And talking of unstable, I've just been down to try and find your old boyfriend.'

'Who?'

'Sorry, I forgot. There've been so many, haven't there? You must get confused.' As soon as I said it, I regretted it.

'Jesus,' she said. 'A bastard is right.'

'I'm sorry. Forget I said that. I was out of order,' I said.

'I suppose you mean Bobby,' she said tiredly, as if it was almost too much effort to speak.

'That's right.'

'And?'

'And he's missing.' I didn't mention that a pair of drumsticks were missing too. I thought I'd said enough already.

'Since when?'

'God knows. A few days. I spoke to his father. But he's not exactly the most reliable witness I've ever come across.'

'I liked him.'

'I think he's probably changed a good deal since you last saw him. They both have.'

'You just want Bobby to be guilty.'

'Sorry, Ninotchka,' I said. 'I know how you feel about him.'

'What are you going to do?'

'Tell the police. Like I should have done last night.'

'To hell with you then!'

I was getting really pissed off with her. No matter what I did I couldn't win. 'What'll make you believe he did it?' I asked. 'A signed confession?'

She didn't answer.

'I'm sorry,' I said for the third time. 'But what can I do?'

'Like I said, go to hell.'

So I went.

First I went to Shapiro's suite. He was there with Lindy, having a spot of light lunch. I asked to speak with him privately, and he took me into one of the bedrooms. When we were alone I asked him one question. At first he refused to answer. So I answered it for him. He was surprised that I knew. But eventually he confirmed that what I'd suspected was true. I thanked him and left them to their pasta with garlic sauce. Then I found Lomax. He was in the bar as usual. I turned down the offer of a drink. *He* confirmed that Turdo had been drum roadie for Bobby Boyle before Boyle left the band. After that I went down to the incident room and found Carpenter and Ripley, and laid the whole thing out for them. Piece by piece.

I told them what Elmo had told me the day before. On the previous Monday evening, he had sold Turdo two grams of smack. It was the first time Turdo had purchased drugs from Elmo. I told them that Turdo had worked for Boyle. I told them what had happened to Shapiro later that night, and why I'd been called in to work for the band. The two policemen were very interested in that particular piece of information. Next, I told them what Shapiro had just admitted to me: that Turdo had given him the wrap that contained, not coke as he thought, but street-grade heroin. The policemen were very interested in that piece of information too. I told them that the smack was identical to the stuff Elmo had supplied to me. I didn't tell them who I was buying it for. I told them about seeing Boyle at the scene of the murder of the security man. I told them about the missing drumsticks, and Bobby Boyle's address in Slough and that he had been missing all week. Finally I gave them Elmo's address. Unfortunately I let slip what I'd done to the happy couple. But I told you, I was very tired.

When I finished I gave them my conclusions: that Bobby Boyle was as guilty as hell of two murders and one attempted murder. Whether or not he was fit to plead was entirely another matter. His motive: revenge.

Carpenter listened to my summing up in silence, and then sent Ripley to put out a description of Boyle on the wire.

Then he about burnt my ears off. He threatened me with arrest for obstruction and wasting police time, and touched on possession of Class A drugs, and GBH on Elmo and Gloria. Then he told me that, if anyone else had got killed whilst I withheld information, I would have been an accessory before and after the fact.

I sat and took it all. I had no choice.

When he finally let me go, I went up to my suite, and went to bed.

To hell with the lot of them, I thought.

27

Of course I couldn't sleep, tired as I was. I just lay in bed staring at the ceiling above me. All of a sudden I fancied a swim. An olympic-sized pool in the basement Lomax had said. But there was a problem. I had no trunks. I telephoned down to the Men's Shoppe and asked for Jeremy. He came straight on the line. I explained what I wanted.

'No problem, Mr Sharman,' he said. 'I'll have one of my assistants meet you at the pool with a selection of swimming costumes in five minutes.'

'Thank you, Jeremy,' I said.

'It's a pleasure,' he replied and we both hung up.

I put on jeans and a T-shirt and slipped my bare feet into a pair of loafers, and went down to the basement. The pool was signposted and standing outside was one of the guys who had brought the clothes up to my suite three days before.

'Mr Sharman,' he said. 'Jeremy sent these for you. Size medium?'

I nodded.

'Any particular style or colour?'

I took a navy blue pair off the top. 'These'll do.'

'Are you sure? Do you wish to try them?'

'They'll be fine.'

'Very well, sir. There are towels and robes in the cubicles. Enjoy your swim.'

'I will,' I said, and watched him walk away before I pushed open the door to the pool. It had a vaulted ceiling and green-doored cubicles stretching away on both sides. The pool itself was big. Olympic sized was right, and totally deserted. The place stank of chlorine and tendrils of vapour rose from the still water. Every sound I made was amplified and echoed around the tiled walls. I walked to the closest cubicle and changed into the trunks. They fitted just right. I went outside and dived straight in. The water was warm and I doggy paddled for a few minutes, then struck out and did one, two, three lengths' breast stroke, the same backstroke. After that I felt pleasantly exercised and floated in the water, almost falling asleep. Eventually I pulled myself out and dried off. I got dressed again and went back to my room, yawning all the way. That time I had no trouble at all getting to sleep.

I woke with a start about five. The room was cool and dark and silent. I thought about my date with Chris Kennedy-Sloane for drinks and a little light conversation about *Pandora's Box*. It seemed pretty irrelevant now, but I decided to go anyway. I had nothing better to do, and my ears were still burning from being bawled out by both Ninotchka and Carpenter. A trip to the City of London seemed to be a decent option.

I took a shower, shaved, and dressed in a suit and tie. By that time it was almost five thirty. I went downstairs and asked the doorman to get me a cab. I'd had drinks with Kennedy-Sloane before and I knew better than to drive. Besides it was rush hour on a Friday evening. I gave the cabbie the address and settled back in my seat and looked out of the window at the other nine-tenths battling their way home after a stressful week at the office.

The cab arrived at the block that housed Kennedy-Sloane & Partners at five to six. I took the lift upwards and presented myself at the reception desk at six on the dot. The receptionist buzzed through to Kennedy-Sloane's secretary. People were leaving for the weekend, and I guessed I'd got there just in time. As if to confirm the thought, his secretary was tidying up her desk, but before she went, she showed me into her boss's office.

It was everything I'd expected and more. Top floor, big picture window with a view of Tower Bridge on one side and the NatWest Tower on the other. Minimalist furniture and a vast expanse of bare, black varnished floor. A bar stocked with more booze than the average pub's saloon bar, and Chris Kennedy-Sloane behind half an acre of desk, empty, except for his feet on the top, talking on a portable telephone. Love it, I thought.

He finished the call with a '*Ciao, bambino*', dropped the phone, swung round on his executive chair, and jumped up to greet me. I looked round again for his benefit. 'Love it,' I said.

'I just knew you would. Come over and have a drink.'

We adjourned to two leather and chrome chairs by the window that looked over the river, and Kennedy-Sloane conjured up two Japanese beers in freezing black bottles. 'You can't get it here,' he said. 'I have it shipped in.'

'Chris,' I said, 'you are a prick.'

'Agreed, but the beer is superb.'

He was right, it was.

When we'd both lit cigarettes, and settled down comfortably, Kennedy-Sloane said: 'So what do you want to know?'

'It's purely academic now,' I said. 'The whole thing's over bar the shouting.'

'How come?'

So I told him. The whole story from first to last. It had all the ingredients I knew he'd love. Murder, mayhem, intrigue. The whole nine yards. When I'd finished he fetched two more beers from the fridge. 'Well, Sherlock,' he said, 'the boy done well.'

'Thanks,' I said. 'But funnily enough, I don't feel very proud of myself.'

'You should.'

I pulled a face and lit another cigarette and looked down at the tiny cars and people in the street below, and envied them. I wished it was me going home to a house and a family and a wife and children and a hot meal and a night in, in front of the TV.

'Cheer up,' said Kennedy-Sloane. 'You wouldn't last a week.'

'What, are you a mind reader now?' I asked.

'I know that look. At least you're not in such a bad way as *Pandora's Box* is.'

'What do you mean?'

'They're in shit. Very deep shit indeed. The band are not doing well at all.'

'I thought they sold records by the truckload.'

'Used to.'

'And they've sold out five nights at Wembley Arena soon.'

'If you believe that, my friend, you'll believe anything.'

'Is that a fact?'

He nodded wisely.

'So what's up?'

'Tastes change. The band has changed.'

'They've been doing that for over twenty years.'

'Getting old maybe.'

'Aren't we all?'

'We're all not in the business of human happiness.'

'Chapter and verse,' I said.

'Simple. Receipts are down. Expenses are up. That little posse spend like money's going out of fashion sometime this evening.'

'I heard they could afford it.'

'They could once.'

'They can now.' I showed him my new Rolex.

'Nice,' he said. 'If a little ostentatious.'

'Chris, I never thought I'd hear you complain at ostentation.'

'Times have changed, I told you. It's tough out there these days.'

'Well, it may be tough out there, but Pandora managed to stump up for over twenty of these suckers the other night.'

'Is that right?' He actually sounded impressed.

'Yup. At ten grand per.'

'Show,' said Kennedy-Sloane. I took off the watch and passed it to him. He took it over to the window. It wouldn't have surprised me if he'd taken off the back and examined the movement with a jeweller's eye glass.

'Well?' I asked.

'It's real,' he said.

'I could have told you that.'

'Over twenty you say.'

'That's right. And you say he's skint?'

'Definitely. The income is drying up. And at least two members are in serious personal financial trouble.'

'Who?'

'Pandora and Box. The founding fathers of the band.'

'What kind of financial trouble.'

'Bad investments and too much blowski. Talking of which, would you…?' He fished a paper wrap from his breast pocket. I was tempted, but I didn't want to get into a long session and end up at 3 a.m. in some hooker's bar with Kennedy-Sloane in full cry. 'Not for me,' I said. 'I'll have another beer. But you go ahead.'

'It's the best.'

'It always is. Next time maybe.'

'Please yourself,' he said, and got up and went to his desk. He opened the wrap and tapped a few rocks out on to the shiny top, and cut them with one of his credit cards. He rolled up a twenty-pound note and took a snort up each nostril, then got two more beers and came back. 'It was unlucky that Shapiro survived the OD,' he said as he sat down.

'Come again?'

'Unlucky for the rest of the band, that is. And anyone with an ear for real music, of course.'

'How come?'

'The best career move right now is for one of them to kick the bucket.'

'Tell me more.' I was interested now.

'When a band like that gets as big as they did, if one of them died, it could spell disaster for the rest. End of story in fact, a lot of times. And the more popular a band gets the more temptation is put in the little bastards' ways, so the first thing you do is to get every member of the band to take out a life insurance policy on every other member. Big ones.'

'How much?'

He shrugged. 'Who knows? A million dollars. Five. It depends.

The premiums aren't cheap, but it's worth it.'

'Is that legal?'

'Perfectly. Tax deductible even.'

'So if someone wanted a quick bob or two…' I said.

'… kill off one of the others,' he finished the sentence for me.

'Precisely. And when the band's on the skids like *The Box* are, it could solve a lot of problems for the rest of them.'

'Cold-blooded.'

'Life in the fast lane is cold-blooded.'

'And *The Box* do live in the fast lane. Someone told me they were the dyingest band in the world.'

'Convenient, wouldn't you say?'

'I sure would.' For the first time I had qualms about Boyle's guilt. But it must have been him, I thought. 'I suppose if you leave the band, the cover would lapse too?'

'Yes. That's written into the policies.'

'So Bobby Boyle wouldn't benefit if any of the others died?'

'No. Anyway, if what you say is true and he gives his royalties away …' His tone of voice told me that he considered the act to be worse than sacrilege. 'I don't suppose he'd be interested in benefiting if one of the others died.'

'I don't think it was money that motivated him. I think he just hates them for kicking him out.'

'Who can blame him?'

'So, Chris,' I said after I'd finished another beer, 'thanks for the info.'

'A pleasure. A great shame that I can't see a way to make a few bob out of it. But still, it's always good to see an old friend doing well.'

'I don't know that I am.'

'You are. Take my word for it.'

'Thanks again. I'll be off now, I think.'

'You won't join me for dinner?'

'No, I don't think so. I'm not in the mood.'

'Another time then.'

'Sure.'

'Soon.'

'Very,' I said.

'Ring me.'

'I will.'

'I'll see you out,' he said, and did. I caught a passing cab, and got him to head back to the hotel.

28

I suppose I got back to the hotel around eight, eight-thirty. I went up to my suite and called Lomax. There was no answer on his number, and he wasn't in the bar or the restaurant. I wondered exactly what my status was now. I was still on wages but the job was over so far as I was concerned. Now it was up to the police to catch Boyle. So did I stay or did I go? I decided to wait and see. I changed into jeans again, made a drink and switched on the TV. I sat down and thought about what Chris Kennedy-Sloane had told me.

Just before ten, as I was waiting for the news to come on, there was a knock at the door. I got up from the sofa and went and opened it. Pandora's two teenybopper playmates were standing outside. Slash was wearing a mini skirt so tiny that I could have used it for a wrist band. It was teamed with a black bra top that left her midriff bare, black tights and shoes. She was carrying a small black suede clutch handbag. The Flea wore black footless tights and high-heeled shoes, and a huge *Pandora's Box* sweat-shirt that had had the sleeves, bottom and neck chopped raggedly with scissors and hung off one shoulder to expose the tops of her tiny breasts. She was obviously wearing nothing underneath. I was looking at prime jailbait, with a capital J and a capital B. 'Hi,' said Slash. 'Remember us?'

'Sure I do,' I said. 'What do you want?'

'Someone to talk to. We're bored. Can we come in?'

I shook my head. 'No.'

'Why not?'

'The place is a mess. The maid service has gone to hell lately.'

'We don't mind.'

'I do.'

'Will you buy us a drink then?' asked The Flea. 'We're all alone.'

'OK,' I said. 'I'll buy you a Coke each. In the bar.' What the hell? I thought. They're just kids, and I could do with the company.

'A Coke?' said Slash disgustedly. 'We want a proper drink.'

'It's a Coke or nothing,' I said.

The Flea crinkled her nose and looked at her sister.

'Slash?' she said.

'OK,' replied Slash. 'Cokes it is. Come on then.'

We took the lift down to the first-floor bar. It was dark and empty. 'Where is everyone?' I said.

Slash shrugged. 'Who knows?'

We went to a booth, and I turned up the small light so that I could see their faces. A barman legged it over and I ordered two Cherry Cokes and a whisky sour for myself. 'We want whisky sours too,' said Slash petulantly.

'The young ladies will have a Cherry Coke each,' I said to the barman. 'Straight. No chaser.'

The two girls looked a bit confused at that, but didn't argue further and the barman left. 'Gotta ciggie?' asked Slash.

'Yes, thanks.'

'Give us one then?'

I shook my head.

'Hell! Why not? No one else cares if we smoke.'

'That's almost certainly the problem,' I said.

'What do you mean?' asked The Flea. 'We don't have no problems.'

'Nothing,' I said. And we were all silent until the drinks came.

'So where's your mother tonight?' I asked when the barman had delivered the order and left.

'Out getting laid, I expect,' said Slash.

Nice, I thought. 'And you're bored?'

'Sure.'

'My daughter suffers from the same ailment.'

'You gotta daughter?' said The Flea. 'How old?'

'Eleven.'

'A baby,' said Slash dismissively.

'Listen to the old lady,' I said. 'I'm surprised you get around without a bath chair.'

They both giggled at that. 'What's your daughter's name?' asked The Flea.

'Judith,' I said. I don't think they were impressed. Not raunchy enough, I imagine. 'What are your real names?' I asked.

'Slash,' said Slash.

'The Flea,' said The Flea.

I shook my head. 'No,' I said. 'The ones on your birth certificates.'

They looked at each other and giggled again. 'Promise you won't tell?' said Slash.

'I promise.'

'Clarissa and Alice,' she said. 'I'm Alice. Isn't that a joke?'

'I like them,' I said.

Her look said, You would. 'Go on, give us a ciggie,' she said. 'I'll only go and buy some.'

'So buy some then,' I replied. 'I'll smoke yours.'

'Give us a fiver for the tab.'

'Use your pocket money,' I said.

She gave me another disgusted look, jumped up and flounced off to the bar, wiggling her backside as she went. She came back with a packet of Marlboro and lit up using a gold Dunhill lighter she took from her handbag. I thought, what the hell again, and had one myself. After all, they weren't my responsibility.

'Where's your daughter now?' asked The Flea.

'With her mother.'

'And you're going out with Ninotchka?'

'Not really,' I said. 'We're just friends.'

'Don't shit us,' said Slash.

'Please yourself,' I said.

'Are you divorced?' asked The Flea.

'Yes.'

'And your wife took your daughter?'

'Yes,' I said again. Although I didn't know why I was discussing my private life with a pair of teenagers.

'Do you see her a lot?' The Flea again.

'As much as possible.'

'What do you do?'

'What all divorced fathers do. Spend too much money on her.'

'Where do you go?'

'McDonald's. The Zoo. The cinema. Round the shops in the West End.'

'Just the two of you?'

'Mostly. When I had a steady girlfriend, she used to come too. But we broke up.'

'Why?' asked The Flea.

I shrugged. 'We just did.'

'Was she nice?' asked Slash.

'I thought so.'

'So now it's just you and your daughter?'

'That's right. You two could come sometime if you like. Judith would like that.'

'But would we like her?' asked Slash.

The Flea shushed her. 'We could handle that,' she said. 'Does she go to school?'

'Of course.'

'I don't,' said The Flea. 'I quit.'

'Sensible move.'

'What bands does she like? Your daughter?' asked The Flea, going off at a tangent.

I shrugged. 'She changes with the weather,' I said. 'But I know she still likes Madonna.'

'Oh, *Maddie*,' said Slash. 'We met her backstage at the LA Forum. She's so cool. And little. She's the same height as me. But built. Boy, I gotta tell you! And guys flip over her.'

'So I believe,' I said dryly.

'She's awesome,' said Slash.

'Have you got a gun?' asked The Flea, changing the subject again.

'No,' I replied.

'How can you be a PI then?' said Slash. 'All PIs have guns.'

'Not this one,' I said. 'I gave them up.'

'Did you used to have one?' Slash again.

I nodded.

'Ever shot anyone?'

I nodded again.

'What's it like?'

'Horrible. About as bad as being shot.'

'Have you been shot?' said Slash, her eyes widening.

I nodded again in the half light.

'I told you,' she said to her sister.

'What?' I asked.

The Flea crinkled her nose again. 'She says you're like Sonny in *Miami Vice*.'

'I've seen every episode,' said Slash excitedly, more like a fourteen year old. 'We've got them all on video.'

'I don't think you're like Sonny at all,' said The Flea. '*He's* cute.'

That put me in my place.

'I agree,' I said.

'Nick's got the same hair,' said Slash. That was the first time either of them had used my name. It made me horny to think of the pair of them discussing me.

'His hair's black, stupid,' said The Flea. 'Sonny's blonde.'

'Apart from that,' said Slash.

I was getting embarrassed, and one of them was playing footsie under the table. I moved my leg.

'Can we sleep with you tonight?' asked Slash. 'We're lonely.'

These two were expert manipulators. I was suddenly ashamed of what I'd been thinking. 'No,' I said.

'Why not?'

'You're too young. And I'm too old.'

'I've slept with loads of older guys,' said Slash. Just the way she said it made me feel even older, if that were possible. And very sad. And pleased I hadn't let them into my suite.

'Are you proud of that?' I asked.

She shrugged.

'You shouldn't be, I'm serious. It's bad for you.'

'Why?'

'Ask your gynaecologist.'

'Who cares anyway?' said Slash.

'I do, if no one else does. When I look at you two I think of Judith.'

'Our mother doesn't mind,' said Slash.

'Then she should be ashamed.'

'She thinks it's kinda cool.'

'It isn't.'

'Keith does too.'

'That maggot should be squashed.'

'Don't you like him?'

'What do you think?'

'He's cool. He buys us stuff.'

'I just bet he does.'

'Will you buy us presents?'

'On your birthdays.'

'My birthday's soon,' said Slash.

'What do you want?'

'Some new lingerie. Sexy stuff. I'll wear it for you.'

I shook my head.

'What then?'

'I'll think of something.' I looked at my watch. It was past eleven. 'Isn't it time you two were in bed?' I asked. Dumb question. I should have known better. They turned to each other and giggled. 'That's what we said already, dude,' said Slash.

'Your own beds,' I said. 'Now get lost.'

'Will you walk us up?'

'No,' I said. 'You can find your own way.'

'Gotta heavy date?'

'No,' I said. 'I'll stay for another drink. Now scat.'

And they went. Much more quietly than I thought they would. They both blew me kisses from the doorway.

I sat in the booth for another ten minutes or so but didn't order another drink. To tell you the truth I felt like shit. Eventually I followed them out, and went up to my own suite. Alone.

29

After all that bullshit I decided to take another swim to clear my head. It had made me feel better earlier, and I thought it might do the same again. So I took my new trunks and went back to the pool.

At first I thought I was alone again. It was steamy and warm inside the pool area with the ever present smell of chlorine and a fine mist like smoke above the water. When I got right inside I saw that I was mistaken. Someone else had decided to take a late night dip. Then I looked again. Something about the picture was badly wrong. I brought it into focus and realised what it was. Whoever was in the pool was fully dressed and very still. Too still. And floating face down just under the surface of the water at the shallow end, arms and legs akimbo, and a halo of long blond hair fanned out like some exotic sea creature. I ran to the side of the pool, kicked off my shoes and slid into the water. It came up to just below my waist. I waded towards the figure and turned it over with some difficulty. It was a he. A he with a soggy plaster peeling off his face. Elmo.

I dragged him to the side and half pushed, half pulled him on to the tiles at the edge of the pool. I jumped out and knelt down next to him. He had no pulse. No heart-beat. I wasn't about to give a junkie mouth to mouth without some protection. Fuck that. We live in dangerous times. I left the body and ran out of the pool area and down the long corridor to the police incident room. It was quiet inside, just a couple of shirtsleeved uniforms present. 'Get an ambulance, quick,' I said to the nearest one. 'You've got a floater in the swimming pool.'

'What?' she said, looking at my bedraggled state.

'Ambulance,' I repeated. 'Swimming pool. Now.'

She hit the phone, and I grabbed the other copper and we ran back to Elmo. The copper brought a first-aid case. He tried mouth to mouth using a protective film. Sensible man. But it was no good. I knew it wouldn't be. After a few minutes he gave up the ghost, sat back on his heels and looked up at me. 'You'd better tell me what happened.'

So I did.

It didn't take long, and as I finished the ambulance crew arrived. They had all the paramedic gear in the world with them, but I knew they were wasting their time. I didn't want to stick around and watch. I asked the constable if I could change into my clothes. He came up to my suite with me. I towelled myself off and put on fresh boxer shorts, socks, trousers and a shirt. As I finished changing Carpenter and Ripley arrived. I was beginning to wonder if they were joined at the hip.

'He was in the pool when you found him?' asked Carpenter.

'Yes.'

'Are you sure?' said Ripley.

'Sure I'm sure. You don't think I put him in there, do you?'

The look on his face said he'd put nothing past me.

'Well, I didn't. And if I had, I'd've made myself scarce. Not gone for one of your people.'

I could tell he wasn't impressed by the logic of that by the way he sniffed.

'Well?' I said. 'Wouldn't I?'

Neither of them answered the question. 'Did you see anyone else around?' asked Carpenter.

'Not a soul,' I said. 'I take it you haven't located Boyle yet?'

'You take it right.'

'Looks like he may be close though.'

'Yes, who the hell knows where he is? But we'll get round to him in due course. When exactly did you go into the pool area?'

'I don't know *exactly*. Five, ten minutes before I saw the constable here.'

Carpenter looked at the uniformed man. 'Eleven fifty-two precisely, sir.'

'And where were you before that?'

'In the bar.'

'Alone?'

'With two other guests,' I said.

'Who?'

'Their names are Alice and Clarissa. They're staying here with their mother.'

'Those two,' said Ripley. 'Bit young for you, aren't they?'

'They were wandering around the hotel alone. I bought them each a Coke and sent them up to their room. Christ, I hope they're all right.'

'We're checking all the apartments,' said Ripley.

Right on cue, someone knocked on the door of my suite and opened it without waiting for an answer. It was another plain-clothes copper. He buttonholed Ripley and took him out of earshot. Ripley looked sick and came over to Carpenter and whispered something in his ear. Carpenter sighed heavily.

'There's another stiff upstairs,' he said.

'Who?' I asked, dreading the answer. As far as I knew Ninotchka was upstairs.

'One of the band. Valin. So that's two. Now you're really in trouble. I told you what would happen if anyone else died,' he said.

He didn't have to rub it in. I felt bad enough as it was. Even if one of them was only a scumbag drug dealer.

'Come on then,' said Carpenter to Ripley. 'Let's take a look.' The pair of them left. I tagged along. I had nothing better to do. Valin's suite was on the top floor next to Ninotchka's. The door was open and coppers were buzzing around like flies. I didn't go inside the room, just looked in between the figures of the policemen. Baby Boy Valin was lying on one of the sofas. Even from where I was standing

I could see that his head was at a strange angle and his face black, with eyes and tongue protruding, just like Turdo's had been. I'd've put money that a guitar string was embedded deeply into the flesh of his neck too.

Oh shit, I thought.

I looked down the corridor to where it doglegged round to Ninotchka's suite, and followed it, and knocked on the door. Don answered. He stood in the doorway, blocking my way. 'Is she in?' I asked.

'Is that Nick?' came Ninotchka's voice from inside.

'Yes,' said Don.

'Let him in.'

Don stood back and I went inside. Big Phil was leaning against the wall by the window. Ninotchka was standing in the middle of the room. She was holding a glass. 'Well, Nick,' she said, 'it looks like you were right.'

'So you've heard?'

'Yes, Phil just told us.'

I looked over at the big man. 'I'm not exactly ecstatic about it,' I said. 'I'm really sorry, Ninotchka.' And I was.

'Poor Elmo,' she said as if she hadn't heard me. 'And Baby Boy Jesus, this is awful.'

I turned to Don. 'Why was he alone?' I demanded. 'Where were your lot?'

He shrugged. 'Don't ask me.'

'If I don't, someone else will.'

Suddenly there was a commotion in the corridor. I went outside and round to Valin's suite again. A uniformed sergeant had arrived from somewhere, and was breathlessly explaining to Carpenter and Ripley that someone had been spotted on the roof.

'We think it's our man, Guy.'

'Mike,' said Carpenter with authority, 'let's go.' He turned to me. 'This time you stay here. You've caused enough trouble as it is.'

I stood and watched as the three of them went down the corridor away from me.

I did as I was told for once.

30

I went back into Ninotchka's room. 'What's happening?' she asked. 'There's someone on the roof.'

'Who?'

I shrugged. 'Who knows?'

She knew. 'Is it Bobby?'

'*They* think so.'

'Oh, sweet Jesus. Let him be all right.'

I said nothing in reply. 'Anyone got a cigarette?' I asked. Big Phil tossed me a packet of B&H. I took one and he lit it for me. I went over to the bar and got a beer. 'Anyone else?' I asked.

No one answered.

I smoked the cigarette and drank some beer and said nothing. Nor did anyone else. Ninotchka paced the floor, still holding her glass.

Ten minutes later Ripley came into the suite. 'Can I see you a minute, miss?'

'Is it Bobby?' she asked.

'Yes,' he said. 'We can't get to him, and he'll only speak to you. No one else. He says he'll jump if you don't go up there.'

'OK,' she said without hesitation.

'Wait a second,' I interrupted. 'He might want to kill you too.'

'No,' she said.

'You can't risk it. He's killed two people already tonight.'

'You don't know that, Nick.'

'I wouldn't bet my life on it.'

'Come with me then.'

'He said just you, miss,' interrupted Ripley. 'There's no knowing what he'll do if someone else goes out there with you.'

'It'll be all right,' she said. I hoped she was as confident as she sounded.

'OK,' I said. 'But stay close to me. Don't let him touch you.' She nodded assent and we went.

Although the suite we were in was on what was called the top floor of the hotel, it wasn't really. Upstairs were the attics of the old houses. A narrow flight of stairs led to them. Up there the dividing walls had not been completely knocked through. The three of us snaked through the gaps, sometimes walking on hardboard, sometimes on thick joists. The attics were dimly lit by dusty bulbs hung high in the rafters, and old pieces of furniture and rubbish loomed through the shadows. The only major work that seemed to have been done was that midget doors had been set in the roof every twenty yards or so, probably where there used to be windows, to allow access to the fire escapes. Carpenter was standing inside one of the doorways. A powerful lamp on a tripod, powered by a battery, shone out onto the roof. 'Thank you for coming,' he said to Ninotchka. And then to me, 'What the hell are you doing here? I thought I told you to stay out of this?'

'If she's going to talk to him, I'm going with her.'

'No, you're not.'

'You can't let her go outside there on her own. Are you mad? It's too dangerous. He might decide to jump off and take her with him.' I saw the look of pain on Ninotchka's face as I said it. 'Sorry,' I said, squeezing her arm. 'But he might.'

'I still don't believe he killed anyone,' she said. I wondered what kind of man Boyle must have been to command such loyalty. And what kind of woman Ninotchka was to give it. For a moment I envied him, and her. 'Two people have died already tonight,' I said to Carpenter. 'Let's not make it three or four if we can help it. I'm going with her, and that's all there is to it. You can't put her in that kind of danger. I'll make sure the publicity kills you if you do.'

If looks could burn, I'd've been toast.

'It'll be all right,' said Ninotchka. 'Let him come with me.'

Carpenter hesitated. 'OK,' he said. 'Now listen, I've got men inside the room under here. When you've got Boyle's attention, I'll call them up.'

'That wasn't part of the deal,' protested Ninotchka.

'Without it, there isn't a deal.'

'So you want to trick him?'

'No, I want you to save him. Whatever he is, and whatever he's done, he'll be better off with us than out there.'

She thought about it for a minute and looked at me. I nodded to her. It really was the only way. 'All right,' she said reluctantly.

'Can't you put a line on her?' I asked Carpenter.

'I don't want a damn line!' she said. 'Heights don't bother me.'

Unfortunately I was remembering just how much they bothered *me*. A line would have made me feel a whole lot better. 'How about the fire brigade?' I asked: 'With nets.'

'He said that if he sees them he'll jump right away,' replied Carpenter.

Christ, I thought, the geezer's thought of everything.

'Are we going, or are we going to stand here all night discussing it?' asked Ninotchka.

I couldn't think of anything further to delay us. I took a deep breath. 'OK, let's go.'

Ninotchka stepped into the doorway. I stood behind her. It was misty outside. It reminded me of the swimming pool, and the beam from the light that the police had set up was haloed with particles of moisture in the air. The green tiles looked slippery and dangerous from where we stood, and our shadows were long and very black on them.

From the door where we stood, slanting downwards to the edge of the roof, stretched a black iron handrail that I imagined led to the top of the fire escape. It was maybe three foot high, and looked very frail. Where the roof finished, it turned sharply along the edges, to the end of the building, where it turned back again for about a yard and ended where it ran into the roof again. In that far corner, in the angle that the railing made, leaning against it was a figure. I could just tell in the refracted light that it was the man who had been in the car park the night before. He was peering down over the edge of the roof checking that no police were coming up. That was why we needed to get his attention.

'Bobby,' said Ninotchka softly. He didn't seem to hear. 'Bobby,' she said again, but louder this time.

He looked up at us with a start. 'Ninotchka,' he said. Then he looked behind her at me. 'Who's that with you?' he demanded.

'A friend. His name's Nick.'

'I told them that you were to come alone.'

'They wouldn't let me.'

'Tell him to go away or I'll jump.' He put his hand on the rail and crouched as if to vault over it.

'No, baby. Trust me,' pleaded Ninotchka. 'He won't hurt you, I promise.'

'Is he a cop?'

'No, I told you. He's a friend. Please let him stay.'

'No tricks.'

'No,' she said.

'You,' he said to me, 'Nick or whatever your name is.'

'Yes?' I said.

'No tricks, understand, or I'll jump.'

'No tricks, Bobby,' I said. But I had my fingers crossed. I'd do anything necessary to get him inside without hurting Ninotchka. There was silence for a moment. I could clearly hear the traffic from the main road. 'Bobby, what have you done?' Ninotchka asked eventually.

He didn't answer.

'Why don't you come in, honey?'

When he replied, his voice croaked. 'They'll put me away again,' he said. 'I couldn't bear it.'

'No, they won't,' she replied.

'Don't lie to me, Nin. Not now.'

'I won't,' she said.

'They beat me up in there, Nin. You'd never believe the things they did to me.'

I believed it.

'I'm sorry, honey,' she said.

'What the hell am I going to do?' he said desperately as if he hadn't heard.

'I don't know. Come in, please. You look so cold out there.'

'I've been out in the cold for years.'

'Come in, Bobby,' I said. 'This is no good for anyone. I saw your dad today.'

'You did?' He looked up again.

'Sure. He'll help you.' Christ, I thought, that was a good one.

Bobby was miles ahead of me. 'Man, if you think that, you didn't see my father. He can hardly help himself to the toilet.'

There was a faint clink from the other side of the roof. Boyle looked down, then at us again. 'Oh, Nin, not you too. I trusted you.' He came up on his hands and knees and crabbed across the tiles towards us. The soles of his sneakers slid away and his hands scrabbled for a hold. I felt Ninotchka move from me and the safety of the doorway. I grabbed her arm, but she knocked my hand down and moved further towards him. I went after her.

Hand over hand she edged along next to the handrail. I was just a foot behind her. Boyle came fully to his feet. They were maybe two yards apart. She let go of the rail, and put her hand out to him. As she did so, she missed her footing. I heard her gasp as she slipped on the damp roof, and both Boyle and I grabbed for her. I caught her wrist and brought her up short. It reminded me of another time and another place. He missed completely, and lost his footing, and his arms windmilled at the air, and he slid down towards the edge of the roof. The backs of his thighs hit the rail, and he stopped for a long second before he toppled over it, arms clutching at the empty air again, and dropped from sight. He screamed as he went until the scream was cut off abruptly with a thud like a bag of damp cement hitting the ground.

Ninotchka screamed too as he went. She tried to pull away from me, but I dragged her back and held her. I could feel her heart beating against me and she sobbed into my chest. Carpenter came out onto the roof and I passed her to him, and when he had her, I went to the top of the fire escape and looked down. Boyle's body lay in a heap on the concrete beneath me. All I could clearly see were his feet sprawled out in the light from an uncurtained window. I gripped the rail with both hands to keep them from shaking. Some policemen appeared from below and knelt over him, then stood and looked up.

The light shone on their faces too, and from their expressions I knew it was over.

31

So that appeared to be that. Apparently Boyle had been living in the attic off and on for a week. A close search revealed a few pathetic belongings: a blanket, some scraps of food he'd stolen from the kitchen, an old copy of the *NME* containing the story that the band were arriving in the country to complete their new album, and a single drumstick. A 2B. The twin of the one that had been hammered into Turdo's chest.

With the death of Valin, *Pandora's Box* more or less fell apart. Box, Shorty Long, Scratch and Shapiro with their respective spouses and hangers-on, and Valin's girlfriend caught the Saturday noon plane for Los Angeles. Valin's body was going to be shipped out after the post-mortem. Nobody seemed keen to stay with it. Pandora made arrangements for his mother to be flown to America for medical treatment within the next few days. His teeny-boppers and their mother were due to accompany him, Ninotchka, Pascall plus wife, and Lomax on the evening plane. The Wembley dates and the rest of the tour were cancelled, and the lawyers, accountants and crew splintered to their many and various destinations.

On that morning I met Lomax in the deserted bar around eleven-thirty. It had the air of a seaside town on the day after the season finished.

I got a beer from the bar and joined him in the same booth I'd met him in days earlier. It really did seem more like months, or even years. He turned up the light as I slid into the seat. 'So that's all she wrote,' he said by way of a greeting.

'Looks like it.'

'Well, this isn't exactly how I envisaged it ending. But thanks anyway, Nick, for all you've done.'

'All I did was get a couple of people killed who shouldn't have been.'

'It wasn't your fault. What do the police say?'

'They're saying nothing to me at the moment. Carpenter is "considering further action", as he puts it.'

'What do you think?' he asked.

'Shit, I don't know. Don't care much.'

'What are you going to do now?'

'Shit, I don't know. Don't care much,' I said again.

'Well, as far as we're concerned, you did the best you could under the circumstances. And we'd like you to accept this.' He took a cheque from his jacket pocket.

'I don't want it,' I said.

'You don't know how much it's for.'

'And I don't want to. Keep it. Send it to Boyle's father.'

'He'll get plenty. All Bobby's royalties revert to him now.' He pushed the cheque across the table.

I picked it up and without looking at the face of it, tore it into four pieces, screwed them into a ball and dropped them into the ashtray. 'No thanks, Roger. It wouldn't feel right,' I said.

'Please yourself.'

'From now on that's exactly what I intend to do. What about you?'

'I'm off home tonight to see the woman I told you about. If she's still there. Eventually the band will get together again. There's an album to finish, remember?'

'Money to be made,' I said.

'That's right. Not everyone has your contempt for the stuff.'

'I heard that the band were broke.'

'Who told you that?'

'An informed source.'

Lomax pulled a face. 'Not really. We'll survive.'

'Even Valin's death, and the tour being cancelled, and the album being delayed?'

'Sure.'

'I believe there were some big insurance policies on him?'

'I'm impressed. You have been doing your homework. There's big insurance policies on each of them.'

'How much?'

'Sterling, two million – two million five. Depending on the exchange rates.'

'And every other member of the band cops that much?'

'Correct,' he said.

'So nobody hurts too much. Except him, of course.'

I saw Lomax shrug. He lit a cigarette.

'So how come he was alone, Roger?'

'What?'

'Valin. How come he was alone last night? Where were all the ever-present security men?'

'Haven't the police told you?'

'I told you already, they're not talking to me at all.'

'He sent them downstairs to wait for him. He was off to a club with his girlfriend.'

'And where was she?'

'He sent her with them.'

'And they all went?'

'Obviously.'

'Strange.'

'Not really. He's one of the stars of the show. He pays their wages. One word from him and they're back on welfare. Look at Ninotchka the other night. She left Don behind and went out with you. You can't protect people who refuse to be protected.'

'Sure,' I said. 'You're right. Whatever. It doesn't matter now anyway.' I paused. 'What time's your plane tonight?'

'Seven. Oh, by the way, you can stay here as long as you like. The place is paid for, for weeks. All you have to do is pay your own bar tab.'

'Thanks,' I said, 'but I don't think so. This place has no pleasant memories for me. I'll go back home, I think. I used to have a cat. Some people down the street are looking after him for me. I'll bet he doesn't even recognise me. So listen, Rog, if I don't see you again, good luck. Say hello to McBain if you bump into him in Los Angeles. It was nice meeting you. Really.'

'Same here, Nick. If you're ever on the coast…'

'I'll look you up.'

'Do that.'

'Goodbye then,' I said. We both stood up and shook hands, and I left the remains of my beer and went back up to my suite to pack.

32

As I finished folding my last clean shirt the telephone rang. I tried to ignore it, but its insistent tone got on my nerves. It just wouldn't stop. Eventually I picked it up. 'What?' I said.

'Nick, it's Ninotchka.'

'Hi,' I said. 'How are you doing?'

'How do you think? Listen, I've got something you should hear.'

'More rock and roll?'

'No.'

'What then?'

'I don't know really, it's strange.'

'How strange?'

'Come up and hear it for yourself.'

'OK,' I said, and hung up.

I put my cases by the door and walked upstairs to Ninotchka's suite. She was alone when she opened the door.

'So what's up?' I asked.

'You tell me.'

She went to the stereo and pushed the play button. I heard the fade to *Zip Gun Boogie,* and then a voice I recognised as Louis Pascall's. '*. . . So when do I get it, Keith?*' the voice said.

'*I told you, it's sorted,*' said Pandora's voice in reply.

'What the hell is this?' I said.

'Just listen and you'll find out.'

'I'm not sure I like the way you operate.' Pascall again.

'You never complained before.'

'I know. But this is starting to get way out of hand.'

'No, man. No, it isn't.'

'I'm not so sure. Roger's brought in this guy Sharman.'

'The guy's a bum,' said Pandora. *'A broken-down PI from the boonies, for Chrissake. Forget him. He's a fucking joke.'*

'He did OK when he worked for McBain.'

'Dumb luck. I said, forget him.'

'OK. But I don't like it.'

'You don't like anything. Except money. The next time I'll do what needs doing. Then the insurance is mine, then it's yours, and I'm in the clear.'

'You know what they say, Keith. Once is cool, twice is queer. If the cops come in and start digging, you're up shit creek.'

'Don't you believe it. I've got the perfect fall guy.'

'Who? Turdo?'

'That jerk! It's the last time I trust him with anything. Getting cheap shit. No wonder it didn't do the job. And now the stupid bastard's guessed. No, I've got someone else in mind.'

'Who?'

'Never mind, you'll find out.'

'You'll screw up the band and the tour.'

'Fuck the tour! We're insured for that too. And I'm the fucking band, don't ever forget that. I've rebuilt it before and I'll rebuild it again.'

'I don't know, Keith.'

'Trust me...' said Pandora, and the tape ended with a click.

I looked at Ninotchka. 'Where did you get it?'

'It was the one we picked up last week. Remember? I just got round to playing it.'

'But how did that get on the tape?'

She shrugged. 'How the hell do I know? Check with Tony at the studio.'

'It's Saturday, Ninotchka.'

'So what? The studio's open. Try it. Otherwise I've got his home number.'

'I will,' I said, and pulled over the phone, got an outside line and dialled the number from Ninotchka's book which was next to it. The phone was answered on the third ring. I asked the switchboard if Tony Tune was in. The operator answered in the affirmative. I told her who I was and got put straight through.

'Tony Tune,' said a male voice

'Tony, it's Nick. Nick Sharman. I came in with Ninotchka to pick up a tape, remember? And I met you again at the reception for *The Miracle*.'

'Sure I remember. How could I forget? Hi, Nick, what can I do for you? I thought I'd heard the last of *The Box* for a bit.' He paused for a beat. 'Oops, sorry, I didn't mean it like that.'

'Sure,' I said. 'Listen, Tony, the tape we collected. When did you do it?'

'How do you mean?'

'When did you make the copy?'

'Let me see,' he said. 'The band came in Monday. That was the night that Trash got sick. Hell of a thing, wasn't it? I knew Bobby Boyle, you know.'

It was hard to be polite. 'Yeah,' I said.

'And you collected the tape when?'

'Wednesday afternoon.'

'Oh, sure. Tuesday night late, then. After everyone else had gone.'

'Like who?'

'Keith and that lawyer guy.'

'Pascall?'

'That's the fella. They came in to listen to some overdubs. I left them to it, and went for a drink. Fucking lawyers! What do they know?'

'You'd be amazed,' I said.

'These days nothing surprises me.'

'Join the club. So it was definitely Tuesday night?'

'Yessir. Well, the early hours of Wednesday, you know.'

'I do,' I said. 'What kind of tape did you use?'

There was a pause. 'Did it fuck up? I didn't have any fresh tapes. That bloody tape-op of mine forgot to order any. Can you believe that? And everything else was locked up. So I used the first one I could lay my hands on. No good, huh?'

'On the contrary. It's perfect. Thanks, Tony. I'll see you later.'

'Look forward to it.' And we both hung up.

I looked at Ninotchka. 'Thank God for incompetent tape-ops,' I said.

'So I was right all along,' she said. 'It wasn't Bobby, was it?'

'Doesn't look like it.'

'Poor Bobby. My God, that bastard Keith! He killed all those people, just for the insurance money.'

I said nothing.

'Are you going to call the police?'

'No,' I said. 'I've been wanting a piece of Pandora since we met. Let's go play him some pretty music. I'll give him broken-down PI from the boonies, the son of a bitch!'

33

Ninotchka knocked on the door of Pandora's suite at precisely one o'clock. Not quite high noon, but close enough.

Louis Pascall answered. He ignored me and said: 'Ninotchka?'

Someone mumbled something inside, and Pascall said, 'Keith says not now.'

'Now,' I said, and straight-armed the door. I caught him off balance, and the door burst open, and I pushed Ninotchka inside. Pandora was the only other person there. 'Just the people we want to see,' I said.

Pandora wore tight jeans and cowboy boots with a western shirt. Pascall was wearing a blue button-down shirt that stretched tightly over his belly, and suit trousers. His jacket was draped over the back of the sofa. There were suitcases lined up neatly on the carpet. Through one of the open bedroom doors I saw two more cases on the bed. On the dining table was a leather Gladstone bag. Open.

'I said, not now,' said Pandora. 'Are you deaf?'

'That's not very hospitable,' I said. 'Especially to a lady.'

'Sorry, Nin,' said Pandora. 'It's been a tough week.'

'Sure, Keith,' Ninotchka replied dryly. 'I understand.'

'I'll see you on the plane later,' he went on. 'We'll talk up a storm then.'

'Let's talk up a storm now,' I said.

'For Christ's sake!' exploded Pandora to Pascall. 'Do I have to take this shit?'

'Why not see what they want?' said Pascall. 'Then they'll go, I'm sure.'

'Now that's how I always thought you rock and roll people would be,' I said. 'Nice and friendly, and lots of fun.' I pushed past Pascall and went straight over to the bar. 'Drink, Ninotchka?'

'Sure. Vodka over.'

I made her a drink and one for myself. The same. The two men stood looking at us.

'Well, now you've got a drink, maybe you'll explain exactly what it is you want?' said Pandora, getting on his high horse again.

'We've got something for you to listen to,' I said.

'Like what?'

'Side two of your new album. Tony Tune recorded it for Ninotchka.'

Pandora looked bored. 'I've heard it before.'

'Are you sure?' I asked.

'Sure I'm sure. Listen, I don't know what you're playing at, but I've heard the album many times and I don't particularly want to hear it again. I'm getting packed if you hadn't noticed. We've got a plane to catch.'

'Your flight's not until seven,' I said. 'You've got plenty of time. Besides, you're a VIP, Keith. You don't have to queue up with the riff-raff, do you? Anyway, I doubt if you'll be catching it. I hope you're insured for a no-show. I'm sure you are. You're very big on insurance, I hear.'

I could tell he was getting annoyed. He wasn't used to not getting his own way.

'I don't know what you mean.'

'Then listen to this.' I took the cassette out of my pocket and held it up for them to see.

'I told you, I've heard it.'

'But this has got a bonus track. Only available on this particular tape. The twelve-inch mix. Yeah, isn't that what you call it?'

'Play it,' said Pascall. It was almost like he knew what was on it. Or at least knew that there was something on it that concerned him.

Pandora sighed but didn't say anything. I went over to Keith's stereo. It was real fancy. More lights than Regent Street at Christmas time. But I figured it out. I put the tape into the machine and ran it back and found the end of the last track.

'So?' said Pandora, as the recording reached the fade out. 'That's the end of it.'

'One second,' I said.

The song finished, and the short conversation began. When the tape deck clicked off Pascall looked well sick.

Pandora carried it off better. 'So?' he said.

'I would have thought it was obvious. You're discussing an attempted murder there. And a murder that was yet to happen.'

'Bullshit!'

'I wouldn't bet on it.'

'I would,' he said.

'You're betting a lot of prison time, Keith, and old Louis there doesn't look any too happy. A couple of hours in an interview room with a hairy-arsed London copper should get him singing better than you can.'

Pandora looked at Pascall. I think he got the picture.

'Own up,' I said. 'You were clever, but you messed up.'

'No,' said Pandora.

'Yes,' I said. 'You got away with it before, didn't you?'

Both Pascall and Ninotchka looked at me. Pandora didn't.

'You killed your bass player in Colorado and stuck his head under a truck. Was he the first?'

'Jackie?' said Ninotchka.

'That's right,' I said.

'Give me a break,' said Pandora. 'You're talking nonsense.'

'Am I?'

'I'd like to see you try and prove it. That was years ago.'

'I don't have to prove it. We have the tape.'

'Tapes can be faked,' said Pandora.

'No,' said Ninotchka. 'The tape wasn't faked, and you know that. Don't you, Keith?'

By this time Pascall was looking like a heart attack waiting to happen. His face was grey, and bubbles of greasy sweat had broken out on his forehead. 'Christ, Keith, I knew this would happen.'

'Shut up, you fucker!' snarled Pandora. 'They can't prove zip.'

'But they can stop us leaving. If the police start more questions, I don't think I can handle it.'

'You prick,' said Pandora, and reached his hand into the Gladstone bag and pulled out a nickel-plated Colt Diamondback revolver with a short barrel and ventilated rib.

'Put that away,' I said. 'Someone's liable to get hurt.'

He stuck it in my direction. 'You,' he said, 'don't move.'

'I'm not going anywhere,' I said back.

'Are you armed?'

'No.'

'You should have been. That was a mistake.'

'Not half as big a mistake as you're making,' I replied. But it was. A lot bigger.

'Search him,' said Pandora to Pascall. He moved towards me. For one moment I thought he was going to step into Pandora's line of fire, and give me a chance.

'Go round behind him,' barked Pandora. Pascall hesitated then did as he was told.

'You'll never get away with this,' I said as Pascall clumsily frisked me.

Pandora smiled. I didn't blame him. The line was out of a thousand bad movies.

'He's clean,' said Pascall when he'd finished.

'So what now?' I said.

'Now you kill Louis and Ninotchka, and then yourself. I'll swear I tried to stop you. I'll be broken-hearted. You loved her, but she loved another. The papers will lap it up.'

Pascall's mouth dropped open. You don't often see that, but it happened.

'Grand opera,' I said into the silence. 'No, soap opera. No one's going to buy that, Keith. Are you crazy?' He didn't answer, but by the look on his face he was. Just a little. Anyone who gets his own way all the time is, I suppose. Maybe disappointment keeps you sane. Or maybe anything can drive you crazy in the end.

'You can't…' said Pascall, and Pandora gut shot him. Pascall looked disbelievingly first at Pandora and then down at the neat hole just above his belt buckle. He touched the wound experimentally, opened his mouth to say something, but just let out a sound halfway between a belch and a moan and fell like a rubber man on to the carpet in front of us. Ninotchka screamed, but cut it off when Pandora looked at her through slitted eyes.

'You've blown it, Keith,' I said. I hope I said it with more confidence than I felt. By my calculations I was the next in line to be dealt with. I just hoped I could get him to talk for a bit and that someone in the hotel had heard the shot.

'No,' he replied. '*You've* blown it. You blew it coming up here. You should have taken that tape to the police.'

That was two mistakes I'd made. Two too many.

'I'm sorry, Nin, I never wanted to hurt you,' he said.

'Thanks, Keith,' replied Ninotchka. 'That makes me feel heaps better.'

Pandora shrugged.

'And more insurance money for Keith. It just keeps rolling in, doesn't it?' I said.

Pandora showed his big teeth in a grin and I dearly wished I'd kicked him in the head the time I'd had a chance. 'So how did it go, Keith?' I asked.

'What do you mean?'

'Did Bobby Boyle come to you, or did you go to him?'

'He came to me.'

'Handy that, the same time that you screwed up killing Shapiro.'

'No. He'd been bugging me ever since we got here.'

'What did he want?' asked Ninotchka.

'His old job back. Drummer with the band. What a joke!'

'The joke was on him, wasn't it?' I said.

'It sure was. He even brought a pair of sticks with him so he could audition.'

'And one of them got hammered into Turdo.'

'That's right.'

'So tell me, did he do the murders or did you?'

'I did of course. Bobby wouldn't hurt a fly. He was just useful to have around.'

'To act as the fall guy. Just like you said on the tape.'

'Correct.'

'But, Keith, if he'd been arrested, don't you think he might have mentioned your involvement? If only in passing?' The bastard was so pleased with himself he only needed the odd prompt to keep him going.

'Are you serious? He didn't know *what* the fuck was going on. He was totally crazed. He was on another fucking *planet,* man. And even if something had got through to whatever he had between his ears instead of a brain, who would have believed him anyway? The guy had been in and out of the funny farm for years. He was a certified lunatic. Who do *you* think they would have believed? All that would have happened was that they'd've stuck him back in the rubber room where he belonged. It was just a bonus you two helped him take a dive. Got him out of my hair.'

Literally the fall guy, I thought. 'A stroke of luck for you really,' I said.

'That's right.'

'Not for him.'

Pandora shrugged again.

'You bastard,' said Ninotchka through bloodless lips, and for a moment I thought she was going to go for him. So did he, and he turned the gun towards her. I caught her arm. 'Don't.' I said.

'Good advice,' said Pandora, smirking.

I ignored the comment. 'And it almost worked too,' I said.

'It's still working.'

'No,' I replied. 'It's all over, Keith. Give up.'

'No, it's not.'

'There'll be too many questions asked.'

'I'll be long gone by then.'

'If you really believe that, then you *are* fucked, son.'

He shook his head. 'Long gone,' he said, again, almost dreamily.

'Keith, what *are* you on?' asked Ninotchka.

'Just his own damned ego,' I commented.

Pandora grunted angrily and his eyes focused as he remembered where he was and what he was doing, and the gun that had been drooping slightly in his hand came up again. That was dangerous. I had to keep him talking. Play for time.

'And it was you that got Valin to get rid of his security and his girlfriend the night he was killed?' I asked.

'Correct again. I told him I had to see him privately on band business, and not to tell anyone else.'

'And then you choked him?'

Pandora nodded again.

'For the insurance money?'

'That's right.'

'But why kill Elmo? What had he done apart from supplying lousy drugs?'

'He sussed out what was going on. Turdo must have said something. Not as stupid as he looked, was Elmo. He tried to put the black on me. Threatened to go to the cops. No chance. He was expecting a nice little bonus that night in the swimming pool. But he got more than he bargained for. And it would all have worked out nice if it hadn't been for you two. Everyone thought him and Turdo were killed by a lunatic with a grudge against the band.

'He was. You,' I said. 'But poor Bobby got the starring role in *that* movie.'

'Right,' he said, and as he did so the outside door to the suite opened and Andrea Batiste walked in. She stood disbelievingly in the doorway looking at us, and Pandora walked over and grabbed her arm and pulled her in. Never letting the barrel of the gun waver for a second.

'What the hell's going on?' she said.

'Just a glitch,' said Pandora. I really think he was beginning to enjoy the whole episode.

Andrea saw Pascall lying on the floor. She pulled away from Pandora's grasp and knelt next to Pascall's body and felt for a pulse. 'He's dead,' she said disbelievingly.

'Your pal Keith killed him,' I said.

She stayed kneeling, looking up at us over one shoulder.

'Just like he killed Turdo, Elmo and Valin,' I explained.

'Keith?' she said.

'Don't listen to his crap,' said Pandora.

'And he'll probably end up killing you too,' I said. 'After he's killed Ninotchka and me.' I looked over at Pandora again. 'It's getting to be too many, Keith,' I said to him. 'Don't you think someone's going to get suspicious soon?'

He bared his teeth in the approximation of a grin again, and shook his head.

'Is this true, Keith?' asked Andrea.

He said nothing.

Ninotchka said, 'Andrea, can't you get him to see that he'll never get away with it? Just let us go, Keith. It's all over.'

Before Pandora could reply, there was a knock at the door. It was getting to be like Piccadilly Circus in the suite. 'Why don't you answer it?' I said. 'It's probably the police.'

Pandora went to the door, still keeping the gun steady. 'Who's there?' he shouted.

'Us,' came the reply. It was Slash's voice.

Pandora opened the door. The two girls came in and Pandora shut the door behind them and leant up against it.

'It's the end of the line,' I said. 'Even you must see that now.'

'He's right,' said Andrea. 'You'd better let them go, Keith.'

'And if I don't?'

'You'll have to kill me too.'

'That can be arranged.'

'And the girls?'

He shrugged. But I didn't think he was quite as confident as he had been.

All I needed was a slight diversion. Anything to break his concentration. Anything so I could get my hands on that damn gun.

'Christ!' said Andrea. 'I knew you were a cold son of a bitch, but I never knew you were this bad.'

'We live and learn,' I said. 'Pascall had to die to learn. How many more before you put that gun down, Keith?'

'Listen to him,' begged Andrea. 'For God's sake, listen.'

'If you don't shut your dumb mouth, you'll be next, bitch,' said Pandora. And made as if to move against her.

And then The Flea gave me the diversion I needed.

'Don't you hurt my mother!' she said, and hurled herself at Pandora like a tiny human cannonball. He slapped her out of the way and I had my chance to make a move. But as I went for him, my left foot, my bad foot, the foot I'd been shot in so long ago, and that had barely troubled me for months, decided to give me one of its timely reminders that all was still not well, and that metal plate can never fully replace healthy bone. As I moved, it shot a stab of pain like a lance of fire up my leg, and I stumbled.

Pandora was quick, I'll say that for him. As my leg gave way, he went back a step and brought the gun round and bounced it off my skull. My head rang like a bell and I hit the deck. Pandora laughed, and pointed the pistol at my head, and The Flea, who had picked herself up off the floor where she'd fallen when he'd hit her, got back into the act. She grabbed his gun hand and sank her sharp white pointed teeth into his wrist and ground her jaw until I think they must have met bone. Pandora screamed, and dropped the pistol and hit out at The Flea with his left hand doubled into a fist. He kept punching her until she released her grip, and still he hit her until she curled up on the floor and lay very still. While this was going on I pulled myself to my feet and went for the gun. But Slash beat me to it. She dived in and grabbed it, moving back out of reach and pointing it in Pandora's and my direction.

By that time we were close enough together and she was far enough away that she could cover us both. We froze. 'Give me the gun, Slash,' said Pandora and held out his right hand. Blood dripped from his wrist and soaked the cuff of his fancy shirt.

'No,' said Slash. 'You've killed my sister, you bastard.'

'She bit me.'

'You didn't have to kill her.'

'She's not dead,' said Pandora. And as if to prove him right, she groaned and moved slightly. 'See,' he said triumphantly. Slash looked over towards her sister. 'You were going to hurt my mother.'

'No, baby, I was just mad. I didn't mean it. Trust me. When this is all over we'll go away together, just the two of us. We'll get married like I promised.'

'If you believe that, you'll believe anything,' I said. 'Trust your sister. She's sussed him out.'

'Shut your mouth,' he spat at me. 'Slash, honey, please.' His tone changed and he drew out the last word as if he was speaking to a baby. Which I suppose he was in a way.

'I don't know,' she said.

She was holding the gun two-handed like Sonny Crockett in every episode of *Miami Vice* that she'd watched on video. I wondered if she knew how to use it.

'Give me the gun,' said Pandora again. And moved one step closer to her.

She bit her lip and shook her head and moved the gun fractionally towards him. He stopped. 'Shoot him then,' he said, pointing at me. 'Shoot him, for God's sake.'

She looked at me, and moved the gun fractionally in my direction. I felt my sphincter tighten. What the fuck was there to know? Point the thing and pull the trigger. That, as Lomax had said, is all she wrote.

'Shoot him, you stupid cow!' said Pandora.

I saw her eyes lock on to mine and I thought it was all over for me. 'He was decent to us,' she said. 'He warned us about you. He said he'd help if we needed it.'

My mouth was dry and I licked my lips.

'Fuck you, you mean,' said Pandora. 'He just wanted to fuck the pair of you.'

'No,' she said. 'He could have had us easy. But he wouldn't. He cared about us. Which is more than you've ever done. He told us about his daughter. He said we could all go out together to the movies or something.'

'He probably wanted you all to have a scene together.'

'No,' she said. And her voice rose an octave. 'No, that wasn't it.' And I could see tears forming in the corners of her eyes.

'Shoot, you silly cunt!' he screamed. 'You'll ruin everything.'

I saw her finger tighten on the trigger and she closed her eyes before she fired.

'Alice, no!' screamed Andrea. But she was too late.

The first bullet hit Pandora in the thigh and exited taking a shower of blood and flesh with it. His eyes widened and he opened his mouth to say something. The second bullet hit him just below his collarbone and sprayed more blood. The third entered his chest and stayed there. The fourth missed him completely, and broke the window behind him. The last bullet made a perfect black hole in his forehead, and took half the back of his skull and a huge hank of his curly blond hair and deposited it on the wall behind him like a small dead animal crushed by a speeding car.

With each shot that hit him he moved a step backwards until the last one killed his motor function, and he crashed on to the carpet.

Slash kept pulling the trigger and even through ears deafened by the gunshots, I counted a dozen or more metallic clicks as the hammer fell on to the empty cartridge cases in the chamber of the gun that she was clutching like she'd never let it go.

Hearts of Stone

by Mark Timlin

The seventh Nick Sharman novel

Life as a private detective has proved too much for Nick Sharman, and when a chance run-in with a couple of young thugs secures him a job as a part-time barman, it looks as if he's found a promising new occupation.

Unfortunately the drug squad has other plans. With two coppers slaughtered in as many weeks, Sharman finds himself being coerced into helping track down the killers.

All too soon he is working alongside a pony-tailed Detective Sergeant with unexpected sexual tastes, and consorting even more closely with a beautiful high-class whore who likes to be spanked… never mind some dangerously unpredictable big-spending villains.

The perils of playing pig-in-the-middle certainly add excitement to life, but Sharman is now mixing with some very bad company, and even he cannot predict the scale of the bloodbath that will follow.

'A fast-talking, hard-hitting hero' – *Time Out*

'Witty, sexy and tough' – *Sunday Times*

'A crackling crime thriller with a great feel for the low life'
– *Manchester Evening News*

'Mark Timlin's is a pure pulp vision. Maybe closer to Spillane than Chandler; his books are bloody romances of the South London badlands'
– **John Williams**, *The Face*